ANNIE JONES

Winner of a Holt Medallion for Southern-themed fiction, and the *Houston Chronicle's* Best Christian Fiction Author of 1999, Annie Jones grew up in a family that loved to laugh, eat and talk—often all at the same time. They instilled in her the gift of sharing through words and humor, and the confidence to go after her heart's desire (and to act fast if she wanted the last chicken leg). A former social worker, she feels called to be a "voice for the voiceless" and has carried that calling into her writing by creating characters often overlooked in our fast-paced culture—from seventy-somethings who still have a zest for life to women over thirty with big mouths and hearts to match. Having moved thirteen times during her marriage, she is currently living in rural Kentucky with her husband and two children.

BRENDA MINTON

started creating stories to entertain herself during hour-long rides on the school bus. In high school she wrote romance novels to entertain her friends. The dream grew and so did her aspirations to become an author. She started with notebooks, handwritten manuscripts and characters that refused to go away until their stories were told. Eventually she put away the pen and paper and got down to business on the computer. The journey took a few years, with some encouragement and rejection along the way, as well as a lot of stubbornness on her part. In 2006, her dream to write for Steeple Hill Books' Love Inspired line came true. Brenda lives in the rural Ozarks with her husband, three kids and an abundance of cats and dogs. She enjoys a chaotic life that she wouldn't trade for anything—except, on occasion, a beach house in Texas. You can stop by and visit at her Web site, www.brendaminton.net.

BLESSINGS
of the
SEASON

ANNIE JONES
BRENDA MINTON

Steeple
Hill®

Published by Steeple Hill Books™

STEEPLE HILL BOOKS

Steeple Hill®

Recycling programs for this product may not exist in your area.

ISBN-13: 978-0-373-81440-4

BLESSINGS OF THE SEASON

Copyright © 2009 by Harlequin Books S.A.

The publisher acknowledges the copyright holders of the individual works as follows:

THE HOLIDAY HUSBAND
Copyright © 2009 by Luanne Jones

THE CHRISTMAS LETTER
Copyright © 2009 by Brenda Minton

CONTENTS

THE HOLIDAY HUSBAND

Annie Jones

To Bob, my everyday husband.

And this will be a sign for you: you will find a babe wrapped in swaddling clothes and lying in a manger.

—*Luke* 2:12

Chapter One

The first time Addie McCoy saw Nathan Browder, he was in children's pajamas.

Not *wearing* them—standing in the middle of a display of them in Goodwin's Department Store. Even if they hadn't been the only two people on the second floor of the aging Star City, Tennessee, landmark store, she'd have noticed him. With his shaggy brown hair, dazzling white teeth flashing against his tanned skin and wearing a royal-blue Hawaiian shirt with gray palm trees against yellow moons, the man stood out.

Having grown up the only child of Bivvy McCoy, sometimes known as the 'Crazy Christmas Lady' for her over-the-top holiday displays in their small Smoky Mountain tourist town, Addie McCoy believed that standing out was vastly overrated. In fact, she went to great lengths to avoid it.

She sighed and looked at the man so totally relaxed even though he was so totally out of place in the dusty old store with dated blue ornaments, sparkly silver snowflakes and bell-shaped mistletoe with pink velvet bows suspended from the ceiling. "Excuse me, sir, but I need to get by you."

He jerked his head up as though he had just realized she was there. He raised his index finger and pursed his lips to panto-mime a "Shh."

Addie froze, unable to take her eyes off the man's raised hand—which she noted had no wedding ring. She opened her mouth to say something more, but he rendered her speechless with nothing more than a wink and a grin.

He motioned for her to join him, holding out his hand for her to take.

A tingle sparked in the pit of her stomach, then shot through her veins. She wanted to resist. She *needed* to resist. Addie did not do things like this. She was not impulsive, and she certainly never did anything to draw at-tention to herself. Besides, it was her first day at Goodwin's, where she had wanted to work since she was a little kid looking into the huge picture windows out front. She had to report to the business office upstairs in a few minutes. But the unexpected invitation came so freely, steeped in fun and secrecy, that she found herself reaching out toward him.

His hand closed around hers.

She gasped at his touch.

He gave her arm a yank to bring her staggering closer, then behind him. After a stealthy backward glance her way, he pointed at a rack of "fun flannel" vintage-print pajamas. Without another sound, he crept toward them.

Her curiosity told her to do likewise, but her head? Well, as the daughter of the town's biggest eccentric—and in Star City that was saying something—she had already had to overcome so much, waited too long and worked too hard to get this job. She had no intention of losing it by being caught playing games with a strange man on the sales floor. She pulled her shoulders back, to physically and mentally wrench herself free of his allure, and asked, "Do you need some *help?*"

Addie strove to never be judgmental. She had experienced that kind of attitude coming from teachers, neighbors and even church members her whole life. And yet she heard herself laying her accent on a little thicker than usual as a means of implying she thought this fellow might want to seek the input of a mental-health professional.

He chuckled, held up his hand to remind her to stay quiet, then sprang sideways out of his half crouch. "No, thank you. I have work to do."

"Work?" Addie jumped backward, clutching her purse to her chest. "Are you—"

"Gotcha!" He yelled loud enough that even with his whole upper body wedged in the rack jam-packed with flannel pajamas, it startled her.

A child squealed with laughter before a small voice cried, "Let's do it again!"

"No deal. Time for fun and games has passed." The man straightened up and looked down. Then, with the kindest expression on his face, he reached in and lifted out what Addie figured was probably the world's cutest little redheaded boy, complete with a hooded sweatshirt, brand-new blue jeans and sneakers with wheels on the bottom.

The man was shopping in the store three weeks before Christmas. Wedding ring or not, clearly he had a family.

"He's very cute." *Not surprising given his hunky dad.* "Um, Merry Christmas to you both."

"No, Merry Christmas to *you*." He held the kid out toward her. "My work here is done. He's all yours."

"Mine?" Her pulse thudded all the way up into her throat. Her brain couldn't quite seem to function. She looked from the man's face to the boy's, then to the man's again. "No! You've got…That's not…I'm not that kid's mother! I'm not even married."

"This isn't the 1950s, ma'am." He studied her for a moment.

"The…?" Her hand flitted from the red-and-green-plaid headband holding back her shoulder-length reddish-brown hair, to the small, rounded white collar peeking from the neckline of the simple black sweater. She shifted her sensible heels, and the knee-length hem of her black skirt swayed slightly. She could just imagine that to a guy like this she'd look like a relic from another era.

He smiled thoughtfully, shook his head and said, "A lot of people have children now without being married. But…"

"Look, I'm a nice Christian girl who is *not* married *or* a mother, and that's certainly *not* my child." She took a step forward, searching the quiet surroundings. "If you want me to, I'll help you find her, though. His mom must be frantic looking for him."

"Hey, Jesse, pal, why don't you go get a drink of water?" He gave the boy a nudge toward the fountain near the elevators.

"Then we'll play hide-and-seek some more, right, Nate?" The boy ran two steps, then went flying down the aisle on his shoe skates.

"Not inside, kiddo," the man called.

The boy groaned but obeyed.

"Sorry to cut you off like that, but Jesse's mom hasn't cared where he was in years, and I didn't think he needed to be reminded of that." He took her by the elbow and guided her to one side, out of the boy's line of vision. "My name's Nathan Browder. Or Nate. I'm the kid's manny."

"His *manny*?"

"Yeah. You know, male nanny?"

"Oh, I know what the word means. I just don't know what to do with the information."

"You do…you do work here, right?"

"Yes, but—"

"Great. Now we're getting somewhere." He clapped his hands together. He took her arm again and spun her toward where the child was still getting a drink, then flattened his large hand between her shoulders and urged her forward. "I left his luggage at the customer-service counter downstairs, and I made lists of the things he needs, his likes and dislikes. As much as I could find out."

She dragged her feet, but the slick soles of her new shoes didn't give her much traction. "Luggage? Likes and dislikes? What are you *talking* about?"

"Okay, Nate!" The little redheaded boy swiped the back of his hand over his mouth, then took off running toward the left side of the building. "See if you can find me again."

"No, Jesse. Stay put. I can't…" Nate looked in the direction of the boy, clearly torn between his own desires and what the child needed from him. Finally, he ran his hands through his hair and sighed. "Duty calls. I'll help you grab him this time, but from then on you're on your own."

"On my own? He's not my—"

"Not mine, either." He narrowed his eyes and lifted his head, listened, then started down the main aisle away from the elevator landing area. "I have a job interview at a prominent private school in Los Angeles on January second. I only took the job escorting the kid here to earn a little extra money until I get that job. I have a plane to catch."

She followed him, not because she was going along with any of this but just to say, "Well, I have a job to do right now."

"Yeah. That job is to help me round up the kid so you can watch over him until your boss tells you differently." He came to an intersection of two aisles and looked both ways.

Addie did the same. The action didn't enlighten her one bit. "My boss?"

"Yeah. Doc Goodwin? Jesse is his grandson."

Addie thought she knew absolutely everything about the Goodwins and their family business. She had never heard of the Goodwins' only son, Darin, having children. "Even if that's true, why would you try to leave the boy with *me?*"

"I don't know anything about the whole custody deal, just that the kid's mom has given up her rights to him and I was hired to fly with him out here, drive him to Star City and deliver him to the top floor of Goodwin's Department Store. I was told they would take it from there."

"The top floor?" Addie looked up at the ceiling. Beyond the glittery, gleaming and mistletoe-decked decorations, she could envision the private offices that nobody could get to without using a special key on the elevator or having someone open the door to the private stairwell along the left side of the building. Doc Goodwin used that staircase to slip from floor to floor in his store. "'Fraid you're a floor short of the top. But don't feel bad. No one would have been free to let you up there this morning because the Goodwins and all the department heads are in a big, important meeting going over the results of the day-after-Thanksgiving sales."

"Sorry. So, you're…?"

"Seasonal temp help. Director of Christmas promotions." She adjusted the oversized crystal snowflake pin on the lapel of her coat as if that were a badge to prove her commitment to the effort. And even though she really wanted to blurt out that she hoped to build a career on these humble beginnings, she held back. Why draw attention to her dismal situation?

"So, do you think you could spare a few minutes to help with Jesse?"

To do a personal favor for the Goodwins? "I'll make the time," she said.

"C'mon then." He moved onto the

carpeted area, threading through the tall racks of robes and gowns.

"Here, Jesse!" As an only child in a town where nobody would have let Bivvy McCoy's daughter babysit their precious darlings, Addie had no experience dealing with children. "Come on out. Here, boy."

"He's not a puppy." Nate looked at her, his eyes teasing. "He's—"

The clatter of plastic hangers caught his attention. He dipped his head and pointed to the tall, circular rack of full-length nightgowns. He raised his finger to his lips again.

Nate pointed to himself, then to her, then to the far side of the rack. He made a semicircle in the air with his finger, then stabbed it toward the side nearest where they stood.

With just that much from the man, Addie knew exactly what to do. In a few quick tiptoed steps, she was in position.

"I guess Jesse has given us the slip," Nate said too loudly. "Nothing more for us to do then but…go!"

Addie dove into the rack.

The metal hooks on the plastic hangers screeched over the rod. A white gossamer-like gown snagged on her headband. She stumbled forward, her hands out. A clunk split the air and a blinding pain resonated through her head.

She cried out, but she did not let that stop her. Her whole life she'd wanted to prove herself worthy of the trust of Star City's pre-eminent family, and she wouldn't let a bonk on the noggin, as her mother would call it, spoil her chance. She squeezed her eyes shut to help the ache pass more quickly, and when her hand met rough fabric and her index finger slid into a denim belt loop, she gave a firm yank. "Don't even try fighting it. I've got you good, and you are never going to get away from me."

"I wouldn't even dream of trying," came the deep masculine voice in reply.

"Oh…" Addie opened her eyes to find her hand on Nate's hip and his face just inches from hers.

She tugged to free her hand, but he moved with her, putting them both in the circle of light coming from above them. He leaned in closer to push her hair off her forehead as he asked, "You okay? We had a real skull-thumper there."

She looked up into his eyes. He seemed to actually care if she had been hurt. "I'm… fine. You?"

He paused only a moment before he cleared his throat and answered, "Fine. Me, too. Also fine."

Addie said, "Well, we better… We still have to find Jesse. And you have a plane to catch."

He tipped his head in agreement, swept the sheer fabric of the nightgown from her hair. "And you have a job to do. So, we…" He stepped back, but only a little. He rubbed the back of his neck, looked down then up, and then a grin inched slowly across his lips. "Look—mistletoe."

Addie followed the line of his vision. Her heartbeat quickened.

"Guess you know what we have to do?"

She couldn't believe this was happening. But why not? She had taken the first step on the path to her dream job, and she would never see this awesomely adorable guy again. She went up on her toes and planted a sweet but firm kiss right on his lips.

"Wow." He stepped back and grinned. "I was going to say we have to get back to work, but that was better. Much better."

He hadn't been asking for a kiss! She was mortified. She was humiliated. She was mad. "Oh!"

She stepped backward, ready to storm off

in a huff, only to have the heel of her shoe catch in the hem of the white gown that had been draped over her. It jerked off the hanger and fell into a pool around her ankle. She shook her leg to free it.

"Here, let me help." Nate reached for her.

"I think you've done enough already." She put her hands on his chest to push him away, but before she could do it two handfuls of silk and lace jerked open behind her.

"What goes on here?" Without even turning to look at him, Addie instantly recognized the voice of short, portly, bald-headed Doc Goodwin. He boomed, "You? What are *you* doing here?"

"This is not what it looks like, Mr. Goodwin." She didn't know how she could breathe, much less speak. Still, she tried to appear calm. "I was just about to go upstairs to fill out the forms to start work today."

"And is this your idea of starting work?" Mr. Goodwin gave her a look that said, given her upbringing, he'd have believed her capable of any kind of wild tale. "I'm afraid you are *not* Goodwin's material, Miss McCoy. You should leave."

Chapter Two

Great. What had started out as a relatively painless means of funding his life before getting that full-time school position had ended up with him caring for an unloved kid and feeling responsible for getting a Southern belle fired. His faith was too strong to leave this unexpected situation without at least trying to make things right. Even if it was near to Christmas—his least favorite holiday.

He stepped out into the open. "Mr. Goodwin, you can't fire this girl."

"I know I can't fire her—she doesn't work for me," the voice called back and the older man trundled purposefully down the main aisle, his bald head high.

"You're not being fair, sir." Nate walked to

the aisle like a man who knew he held a trump card and was not the least bit afraid to use it.

"I can speak for myself, thank you." The woman pushed past Nate, her shoes clip-clopping briskly after the uneven gait of the old man lumbering down the aisle, then turning left. "Mr. Goodwin, please, let me explain."

"I don't need an explanation, Miss McCoy," the gruff voice bellowed back. "Not from you or your slacker boyfriend."

"That…that *man* is *not* my boyfriend." She stopped, folded her arms, then glared at Nate. She took a step toward him, and the shoes that made her look a bit like a kid playing dress-up slipped on the slick floor. She wobbled.

That seemed only fair. The minute he had looked into those eyes inches from his as she stood with a nightgown draped over her hair like a wedding veil, he had been thrown off balance. "I don't think he's listening."

"My whole life I looked forward to the day I'd have a quiet life here in Star City. I imagined a simple little house that looked like every other house on the block. I imagined that I'd belong to the church choir, I'd join the PTA, work on committees, fit in with the community. I know it doesn't sound like much to a guy headed for a big job in Los Angeles, but it's all I ever wanted, all I dreamed about. Working here was a part of that dream." She finally took a breath, and her shoulders slumped forward. "And I just lost it forever."

A guy didn't have to have a master's degree in human behavior to recognize a sweet girl who just wanted to be accepted, who deserved to be given a chance to do her best, who needed a break. As his last official act as manny to Jesse Dylan Moberly Goodwin, Nate was going to see to it that she got that break. "Don't be too sure about that lost dream, Miss…"

"McCoy. Addie McCoy," she murmured.

"Addie McCoy," he repeated softly. He smiled and extended his hand. "Nice to meet you, Addie McCoy."

She took his hand. "Nice to meet you, too, Nate Browder."

"Don't give up on your dream just yet. Christmas is coming. It's the season when the most unexpected things can happen." He went to her side and glanced down the rows of sleepwear to where the older man had almost reached a gray metal door with a lit exit sign over it. With his eyes still on her, he called out to the old man again. "Miss McCoy here was not fooling around on company time."

"That's not what I saw," the man blustered without even turning to look at them.

"What you saw was a good employee doing a good deed. She was just helping me to entertain and take care of your—"

The elevator bell, about ten feet away from them, dinged.

Nate winced and pressed the heel of his hand to his forehead. "Jesse!"

"Jesse," Addie echoed in a softer tone but just as urgently as he had spoken his charge's name. She spun around and, suddenly completely unconcerned with her own problems, started walking in a circle around the nearest rack. She bent down, then stretched up on tiptoe. "He's probably hiding in the clothes racks laughing about all this. I'll help you find him."

"Did you say Jesse?" That had Goodwin's attention. He turned and started back toward them. "I haven't seen the child since he was three or four. My son was only married to the boy's mother for just over a year. I thought they were sending someone along to deal with him."

The elevator door whooshed open just as Addie came around the rack, ending up at Nate's side again. He stopped her with just a touch to her shoulder and a resigned look as he called out to Doc Goodwin. "They *did* send someone. Me. Only I haven't done such a great job."

"I believe you have misplaced something, Mr. Browder." Maimie Goodwin, all six feet two inches—including heels and a coif of lightly teased silver hair—of her, stepped out of the elevator with a scowl on her face and a small redheaded boy in tow.

Poor kid. Nate wanted to go to him and give him a great big hug and tell him everything would be all right. But Nate couldn't exactly promise that, could he? His job here was done. He had a plane ticket and a job interview in California.

Like Addie McCoy, this was a kid who could have greatly benefited from an early Christmas gift—a second chance. Everybody needed one of those now and then. Given Jesse's history and the looks on the faces of the elder Goodwins, that was not going to happen.

Jesse looked up. His lower lip quivered.

"Guess you won the last round of hide-

and-seek, buddy." Nate gave the boy a thumbs-up in an attempt to encourage him as much as he could. "Good job."

"I wish I could say the same to you, Mr. Browder." Mrs. Goodwin led Jesse out of the elevator.

"Don't blame him, Mrs. Goodwin." Addie McCoy stepped between Nate and the elegant woman guiding Jesse by keeping one manicured hand on his shoulder. "He only lost track of Jesse for a minute, and that was just because he was trying to help me get my job back."

The elevator doors rattled shut. Mrs. Goodwin tipped her head to one side. "What could Mr. Browder possibly do to help you get your job back, Addie, dear? Pay your salary? Volunteer to play Santa Claus himself for free? I don't think even that would change our minds."

"About me?" Addie asked in a small voice that went straight through Nate.

Mrs. Goodwin shook her head. "About closing the store after the first of the year, my dear."

"What?" Nate had never even heard of Goodwin's Department Store or Star City, Tennessee, until ten days ago, and suddenly even he was shocked and dismayed by this news. He looked at Addie, suspecting she was the reason for this sudden onslaught of sympathy. One look in her shocked and misery-filled eyes, and he couldn't keep himself from offering, "If playing Santa Claus for free would help, Addie, I'd do it."

Doc Goodwin gave a blustering harrumph, then came up to join them, his head bowed. "I'm sorry I allowed you to think I was letting you go because of something you had done, Miss McCoy. It was a lapse of pride on my part."

Addie shook her head. She looked like a kid who had just learned Christmas wasn't coming this year…maybe not ever again. "I don't understand."

"That was the conclusion of the meeting we just had. We have to start making cutbacks immediately, starting with suspending all Christmas promotions." Mrs. Goodwin glanced down at the glum-faced boy at her side, pursed her lips, then placed her hands on either side of his head, covering his ears as she whispered, "We just had to sack Santa Claus."

Doc shrugged his large, sloping shoulders. "I should have been up-front with you about that."

"Yes, you should have been." Maimie dropped her hands from Jesse's ears, then dipped her eyes to indicate the child. "All of the problems we're dealing with today could have been avoided if everyone had only been up-front and honest from the get-go."

Addie's eyes shifted from Jesse to Maimie to Doc and then to Jesse again. Nate could tell she *so* wanted to ask what the older woman meant by that. But she didn't. Nate found that level of unselfish respect and kindness endearing.

Mrs. Goodwin must have felt a touch of the same emotion as she smiled, sort of, raised her head regally and said, "And it is in the spirit of openness and honesty, Addie, that I will tell you that I would like to offer you another position with the store—"

The girl's lovely face lit up. She glanced at Nate, smiled, then gushed, "Oh, Mrs. Goodwin, that would be so—"

Maimie held up her hand. "But I can't. We have more people on the payroll than we can afford right now. And with all the competition for the tourist dollar these days? Well, our type of store just doesn't pull the people in, even at Christmastime, anymore. I'm sorry."

"That's okay, Mrs. Goodwin." She looked so sad and so small as she twisted and tugged slightly at the almost garish snowflake pin on her lapel and tried valiantly not to cry. "I just wish there were a way I could help."

"You can help by not telling anyone what you heard here today," Doc suggested a bit gruffly. "If people find out the store is struggling and may close, more than a few of them will decide to shop elsewhere."

"Yeah. I know." Addie nodded, then looked at Nate. "We've had a lot of stores come and go in town. But Goodwin's has always been a staple. One of the few things in my life, besides my faith, that was consistent and reliable."

"What's going on?" Jesse demanded. "You look like you dropped your handheld game system in one of those wishing fountains."

The Goodwins looked to Nate to translate.

"There was an incident at the airport," he explained. "I told him to ask Santa for a new game system, by the way. I hope that's okay. If it's a problem…I mean, if Santa doesn't come through, I'd be happy to get him one. It seemed to mean a lot to him."

"That's hardly in your job description." Maimie sighed, then looked at the boy. "We can still afford whatever we decide the child needs."

"Yeah, but…" Nate looked at all of the faces staring back at him.

Each one of them was dealing with his or her own particular brand of broken heart, and at Christmastime, to boot. Not that Nate had ever felt any real affinity toward the season. As the child of divorced parents who alternately tried to outdo one another or, as he got older, tried to dump him on each other, he considered it one of the lousiest times of the year. No wonder he used to stay at college for winter break. Nowadays, he just wanted to run away from anything that reminded him of the myth of there being no place like home for the holidays, surrounded by the love of family and friends.

"Doc, why don't you take the boy to the toy department and let him pick something out?" Maimie suggested.

"Wow, can you do that?" Jesse asked, his whole face brighter.

"I still own this store, young man." The older man plunked his chubby hand on the kid's shoulder as he began to guide him to the stairwell. "I can do anything." He glanced back at Addie a bit glumly and added, "Well, *almost* anything."

"I promise you, Miss McCoy," Maimie was quick to chime in, "If I can think of any way that we can bring you on board at Goodwin's to our mutual benefit, I will do it."

"I appreciate that more than you know, Mrs. Goodwin," she said in her soft, lyrical accent. The two of them began to walk toward the elevator.

Nate had felt sorry for these people? At least they'd have each other and the comfort of a familiar hometown full of traditions and support. What would he have?

Only everything he ever wanted. Christmas alone where no one could find him. A job making loads of money catering to kids who didn't really need him for anything. Freedom. No one to disappoint him, and no one to be disappointed in.

That's what awaited him. It had seemed like more than enough for a great life when he'd left California. Now, having come to Star City, having to leave Jesse and having met Addie McCoy? It felt less like a dream life and more like a life he was settling for.

Chapter Three

Goodwin's closing? Ten minutes later, Addie stood on the corner at the end of the block clutching a Goodwin's Department Store gift certificate that might not be any good a month from now. Mrs. Goodwin had given it to her as an apology.

Please, God. She sent up a quick, heartfelt prayer. *Don't let this happen. If they close, I don't know what I'll do.*

Even if they *didn't* close, Addie didn't know what she would do. She had no plans for the rest of the day or, now, the rest of her life. Just a sick feeling in the pit of her stomach about how her mother would react when she came home from her own job tonight to find Addie sitting gloomily in their darkened, silent house. She rubbed her temple. If only she *could* sit in a darkened, silent house.

Not possible. Not this time of year. From the weeks before Christmas until the day after New Year's, the McCoys' rectangular box of a tract house was anything but dark or silent. Thousands of twinkling lights set to flash in time with a blaring assortment of Christmas music hung from every tree and eave. A manger scene lined in rope lights behind a nine-figurine blow-mold lighted Nativity took center stage. Dotting the lawn were giant inflatable characters and painted wooden cutouts flooded by spotlights. And on the roof an animated Santa that turned, waved and bellowed "Ho ho ho," all of it plugged into a computer-regulated timer set to start up a half hour before dusk.

Every year her mother added something new to the chaos. And every year Addie dreamed of the day she would move out and celebrate the season in peace.

"Not this year," she muttered, staring at the gift certificate. But her sadness was less for herself than for Star City losing the store that had meant so much to so many. And what about the Goodwins? What would they do?

"We'll pay you!" Mrs. Goodwin's voice

carried the whole half a block from the front door of the old department store.

Addie spun around to see Nate Browder politely holding one of the twin front doors open for Maimie while she stubbornly stood holding open the other one.

"No." He let his door fall shut. Slipping on a pair of black sunglasses, the sunlight glinting off the gold highlights in his wavy brown hair, Jesse's manny took long, purposeful strides in Addie's direction, though he did not seem to see her. "I can't reorganize everything because your son failed to make adequate arrangements for Jesse."

"Flights can be rescheduled, Mr. Browder. We will cover the costs and throw in a bonus." Maimie kept pace with him step for step. "You took this job. You are the boy's caregiver."

"I took a temporary job to get the boy to Star City. He's here. My work is done. It was nice meeting you, but I have to go." He pointed in Addie's direction.

She looked away quickly and began to press the walk button frantically, hoping they'd think she had simply been standing there waiting to cross the street.

"I'm parked on the next block, to protect

your family's privacy," he said. "I *had* hoped to bring Jesse in and get out without drawing too much attention."

If he meant that as a hint that she should probably retreat, Maimie did not take it. "And I had hoped you'd bring Jesse in and stick around to take care of him without drawing too much attention."

Addie glanced around. On a warmer day in better times there would have been a dozen folks standing nearby riveted to the goings-on. Today the only witnesses were Addie and a few shopkeepers with their noses practically pressed against their own glass doors. Still, she felt bad for Mrs. Goodwin.

"Doc and I are trying to keep a business afloat here, Mr. Browder. We have limited time to devote to a child. Whereas you…" She reached for his arm to hold him in place.

Just then the small redheaded boy clutching a plastic superhero figurine in one hand came outside to stand and watch Doc take the See Santa Here poster out of the front window.

"You can't just walk out on him now." She shifted her stance to make sure both she and Nate had a good look at the heart-wrenching sight. "Not at Christmas."

Nate stopped and looked back over his shoulder.

"Stay." Addie whispered the choice she wanted him to make. Not for herself, of course. It was the choice anybody would have wanted him to make, looking at that kid and knowing the Goodwins were in a fix.

He shook his head and began walking toward the corner again. "Jesse is *your* grandson, Mrs. Goodwin."

"Stepgrandson," she corrected him, following again. "Actually, technically, my *ex*-stepgrandson."

Addie gasped at that news, then realized they now knew that she'd been eavesdropping. Though, in her defense, most people would not have considered listening when two people were shouting at each other as they walked down the street eavesdropping.

Nate gave her a wink that made her feel excited and self-conscious at the same time. Maybe it was a good thing he was leaving, she decided. Enduring her mother's high-profile version of Christmas cheer would be hard enough without trying to hide her interest in a man who had no intention of hanging around.

He kept moving as he spoke over his

shoulder to the woman dogging his heels. "It doesn't matter what you call him, Mrs. Goodwin. He's still your son's legal responsibility."

"But my son doesn't really know this child."

The light changed. Nate hesitated a moment, looked as if he wanted to say something more, then held up his hands in surrender and headed toward his car.

It wasn't what Addie had expected. Of course, she didn't have any business expecting anything at all of the man, but she had hoped he would change his mind. She guessed Star City and a kid with nobody else to count on couldn't hold a candle to his big plans.

"Besides, my son isn't even in town," Maimie called after Nate before turning to Addie. "He's off on his honeymoon, for his second marriage."

This is the place where you step up and volunteer to take care of Jesse, Addie told herself. Only she knew that the Goodwins would never allow her to do it. She had a marketing degree and a mom that didn't know the meaning of the word discreet. Not exactly the kind of person you wanted handling this kind of delicate family situation.

Unless you were totally desperate.

"Excuse me, Mrs. Goodwin. I couldn't help overhearing about your son and Jesse and Nate having plans and—"

"Plans? Don't tell me about plans, young lady." The older woman shut her eyes and bowed her head. "When I was your age, Addie, and Doc was probably not much older than Mr. Browder there, we had such grand plans. They certainly didn't involve a twice-married son finding himself responsible for a stranger's child."

"Lots of people thrive in blended families, Mrs. Goodwin," she said, trying to accentuate the positive.

"Oh, Addie, dear. That's sweet, but clearly you can see the Goodwin family is less blended than just plain mixed-up." She gave Addie a pat on the shoulder.

Nate started the engine of his rental car.

"It's just not the same world it was when we opened the doors of Goodwin's fifty years ago." Mrs. Goodwin looked in Nate's direction, her face pinched with worry. "You could count on people then, and people, at least the ones in and around Star City, could count on Goodwin's."

"I know that was true in our family," she assured the older woman. With that she put her back to Nate. Any moment she'd hear him roar off, which was for the best, of course. Why would she want a guy like that to stick around, anyway? A guy who would leave an adorable kid and a kindly and stressed-out set of grandparents in the lurch, and at Christmas?

"You know, my parents swore we'd never make a go of the store, but Doc and I understood what families needed." Mrs. Goodwin had gone all gooey and sentimental as she stood back and gazed lovingly as Doc came outside to collect Jesse. "It was just a matter of showing them how good a Goodwin's life could be."

Addie watched as the old man in his dark brown business suit offered his hand to the little boy in brand-new dark blue jeans. "Good at Goodwin's… Didn't that used to be the marketing slogan?"

"You *have* done your research." Mrs. Goodwin smiled. "Come see how good a Goodwin's life can be. Not only was it our motto, but our very first Christmas ever, it was the basis for a publicity stunt that had the Goodwin name on every tongue in Tennessee."

"Whatever that is, maybe you should try

it again!" *And maybe you should hire a girl
with a brand-new marketing degree who
clearly does her research and desperately
needs a job.*

Addie paused for a moment to listen. The
engine of the lone running car parked on the
next block was still purring in the quiet of
the late November morning. She tried to
ignore that and what it could mean.

In front of Goodwin's, Jesse rejected his
ex-stepgrandfather's hand but in a split second
had lowered the wheels on his shoes, then
nabbed the tail of the old man's suit jacket.
Jesse went gliding along behind him, laughing
as Doc pretended to try to shake him off.

A big marketing ploy. Not even knowing
what it might be, she knew she was so much
better suited to that than to playing nanny to
a little boy.

Addie presented herself with cool but
forceful enthusiasm and said, "I'd love to
help you re-create that first publicity stunt,
Mrs. Goodwin. You said if you could think
of anything you could hire me for, you'd do
it. This seems like a win-win situation for us
both. You take a chance at stirring up big
sales numbers for Goodwin's this season,
and I get a chance to prove myself to you,

or to whoever I send my resume to if Goodwin's doesn't...need me come the first of the year."

Maimie stood back and gave Addie a long, slow, squinty-eyed going-over.

Addie tried to look professional, fearing that in her old-fashioned outfit she might actually seem plain and unimaginative instead. Maybe she would have been wiser to offer to take care of Jesse. Though looking at the boy playing with Doc, she wondered if they would actually have a need for a full-time nanny. Even if they did, that would only be until their son returned from his honeymoon.

"I can do this, Mrs. Goodwin. I know I can." In that moment, she became aware that the car's engine had stopped. Or perhaps while Addie had been making her big pitch Nate had merely driven off. Not that it mattered, of course. Jesse would be fine without him, and it wasn't like Addie needed him for anything. She had a plan, and that plan was back on track. "Just tell me what I need to do."

Maimie smiled slowly. "It's not what you need to *do* but what you need to have that would be the problem, my dear."

"I have the degree. I have the energy. I've

done the research on the entire history of Goodwin's. What else could I possibly need?"

"A husband. Or at the very least a man to play the role. Nothing long-term, just some-one to act as your counterpart for one or two weeks."

"Wait a minute!" She tried to make sense of that statement. She played what she had just learned against all the newspaper clip-pings and local stories about the old store. Addie's face went hot as it dawned on her what the older woman was talking about. "You don't mean…Mrs. Goodwin, the first publicity stunt wasn't the year you had a couple living in the front window of the store using only things for sale at Goodwin's for the two weeks before Christmas?"

"Twelve days," she corrected.

"I'd be happy to do the behind-the-scenes work for that, but I don't think…" She could hardly breathe. Her whole life she'd longed to disappear and just be one of the crowd. Her stomach churned. "Mrs. Goodwin, I *can't* put myself on display like that."

"Then I can't give you a job, dear." The woman reached out, took her hand and gave it a pat. "I can't pay for you to run the pro-motion and someone else to man it. Sometimes you have to be willing to stand up and let the world know what you believe in."

Despite the warmth of the sunshine reflecting off the sidewalks and large plate-glass windows, a chill snaked down Addie's spine. This was it. She had always wanted to work at Goodwin's, and now not only was she being offered a chance, but if she didn't pitch in and do her part, there might not be a Goodwin's to work at ever again. "I guess I could do it, but I wouldn't have the first idea where to find a husband, not even a fake one."

"Okay. I'll stay. One, two days tops, more if I have to, but not longer than a week. I absolutely have to be gone by Christmas Eve," Nate shouted as he crossed the street toward them. "But the second you find someone else who can take my place, I am outta here."

"Good to hear it, Mr. Browder." Mrs. Goodwin gave Addie's hand a conspiratory squeeze. "This may just be the answer to all our problems."

Her heart pounded. "You mean to take care of Jesse, right?"

"To *help* take care of Jesse, yes, until my son returns next week. That will give you time to get the word out and make preparations for the publicity stunt, and then…"

"And then…?" Addie watched the handsome man she had impulsively kissed as he reached her side.

He looked even cuter standing there with the breeze ruffling his hair, and his heart—putting Jesse's needs ahead of his plans—on his sleeve.

"And then *what*?" he asked, slipping off his sunglasses and looking first in Maimie's eyes, then Addie's.

"And then we're going to give you a chance to do what so few people ever get to do." Mrs. Goodwin slipped her arm into Nate's and began to lead him back toward the store. "We're going to give you the opportunity to actually follow through on your promise to Addie."

"What promise?" he asked, looking back at Addie.

Maimie gave him a yank to keep him by her side as she said, "That you'd happily help out if it would get her her job back."

His loafers scuffed along the sidewalk as he glanced back over his shoulder at Addie again. "Do you know what she's talking about?"

"Unfortunately, I do, and I want you to know—including you was not my idea."

Chapter Four

They stepped into the elevator on the first floor of the nearly empty department store. Mrs. Goodwin and Addie had not stopped talking the whole time the three of them made their way in from the street. Nate didn't mind. Not one bit. He enjoyed listening to Addie infusing every last word she uttered with enthusiasm and her soft Southern accent.

He could get used to that, he thought, and just as quickly reminded himself that he'd better not let himself get too comfortable with that voice, with those dreams, with this girl. He had plans. He had worked long and hard to get a chance to…

He paused as they walked through the main aisle and he caught a glimpse of Jesse running his hand on the red satin arm of the painted gold chair where the store Santa was supposed to be. Something in that gesture really got to Nate.

Of course it did. He had been that kid who knew not to rely on a mythical character for the answer to his hopes and yet couldn't help but wish that somebody would help him get the one thing he wanted most in the world. A real family.

Doc Goodwin noticed Jesse's longing. He bent down and spoke to the boy, who nodded then cocked his head and whispered something to the stout bald man.

That's all Nate ever really wanted to do. To help others, to help kids in the way he had never had anyone help him. Deep down he knew he wasn't going to get that at the posh L.A. school where he had landed his one and only job interview since finishing his doctoral degree last spring. Maybe it was a good thing he was staying. Maybe it was worth a few days' vacation and enduring a little holiday cheer if it meant Nate had a chance to make a difference in Jesse's life. And Addie's.

He turned his attention to her again. She smiled broadly and said, "What do you think?"

He thought he should have been listening more intently, but the women really hadn't gone to great lengths to include him. Under other circumstances he might have been tempted to just smile and tell them it sounded great but…

He looked at Santa's chair again and remembered his promise. No matter how much he wanted to help, he couldn't see himself, a guy who really didn't care for Christmas, playing Santa. So to make sure that didn't happen, he just asked outright, "What's my role in all this?"

A few minutes later Nate sat in the offices on the top floor of the Goodwin's Department Store building. Doc was still keeping Jesse occupied until he and Maimie got the details extending Nate's work as the boy's manny worked out.

Addie had slipped out of her coat and was hanging it up on a row of hooks on the wall, just like a dutiful employee settling in for a full day's work. Though he did think she was taking a little too much time messing with her coat collar trying to get it just right, maybe. Or maybe she was just trying to make herself unobtrusive in the austere office while Maimie Goodwin made the case for his participation in this unconventional publicity-stunt idea of theirs.

"You said you'd go so far as to dress up as Santa Claus in order to help Ms. McCoy keep her job." Maimie paced slowly from one end of the large cherrywood partner's desk to the other. "If you think about it, what we're asking isn't nearly that drastic."

"Or at least not as potentially itchy." Addie turned from her coat. Something silver and sparkly but also white and glittery was cupped in her hand as she rubbed her knuckles along her cheek. "You know, with the fake beard and all."

"Well, you got me there. That's generally what I look for in temp work—a low itch factor." He frowned. The truth was that he'd been far less picky than that about the kind of temp work he'd done to supplement his way through college and grad school. Dishwasher. Blood donor. Amusement park ride operator. But with his future on the line and the reality that he couldn't look for aid to either of his parents, who now had new families to support, he'd been highly motivated then.

Not that there weren't certain motivations to do this. He looked at Addie practically trembling in her grown-up girl shoes as she struggled to fasten her snowflake pin she must have just retrieved from her coat onto her sweater. All the while she kept her eyes trained on him.

She needed a break. Nate had always espoused the virtues of making your own breaks. Wasn't that just what Addie had done?

"Oh!" Her hand suddenly jerked back, sending the pin flying to the floor by his chair. "Little mishap," she explained with a nervous laugh as she rushed to pick the trinket up again.

He bent down to rescue the Christmas object for her as he shook his head. If she could propose this wild idea to a total stranger, surely she could find somebody else to do this with her. Why him?

"It has to be you," she whispered as they both reached for the pin on the floor and her mouth was just inches from his ear. "It's a small town, Nate. If we find a local guy to do this, people will get the wrong idea."

"I see." He scooped up the cold metallic snowflake and placed it in her open palm.

She glanced down to fasten the snowflake onto her black sweater, then raised her head to look deeply into his eyes. "Thank you."

He had said "I see" not "I'll do it," but as he looked into those big, clear eyes shining with hope and gratitude, Nate couldn't help believing he had just made a commitment—one that he would do everything within his power to keep.

Chapter Five

"Have I told you lately just how proud I am of you?"

"I haven't really accomplished anything yet, Mom." Addie looked up from the bowl of cold cereal she had been eating over the kitchen sink.

"You've accomplished more than a whole lot of people, sweetie. You found what you wanted in life, and you worked and studied and found a way to make it happen. Even if it doesn't work out the way you had always hoped, you took a shot."

She smiled as her mother, dressed in a pink-and-yellow chenille bathrobe, with her platinum-blond hair wrapped in curlers, took a seat at the vintage-style chrome-and-turquoise Formica table. Holding a cup of coffee the size of most soup bowls in one hand, the older woman propped up her pink caribou feather mules on the chair across from hers, then clicked the computer mouse to make the flat-screen monitor spring to life.

"I guess I learned a few things from my mother," Addie teased lovingly. "I can't believe you developed your own Web site and blog just to put our house on the Internet."

Bivvy took a sip from her cup. "Wave to the people, darling."

Addie stepped back from the sink, mortified. "People can *see* me?"

"I added a live Web cam this year."

It was still dark outside. Dark everywhere except the McCoys' front yard, that is. There the electric radiance shone in through the small window over the sink to illuminate Addie's simple black-and-white outfit and uncomplicated breakfast fare with a green-then-red-then-blue-then-amber glow.

"No one can really see you, but if you wave they might be able to see some movement. Try it and I'll let you know." She pointed toward the window, one hot-pink acrylic nail glinting in the light from the computer screen.

"No." Addie curled her bowl close to her

body and shrank back another step. "Mom, that is an invasion of my privacy."

"Sweetie, the camera takes a long, wide shot. You can't see the doors or any windows but that small one right over the sink. I don't think, if a body didn't know it was there, that a person could see it." She snapped her fingers. "Now wave and let me see for sure."

Addie set her bowl down, spun on her heel and headed for the bedroom.

"If you can't do this, how are you ever going to put yourself on display in Goodwin's windows?" her mother called out from her spot in front of the computer.

Addie stopped in the hallway. "I am just doing a few recipe and craft demos during working hours, Mom. No big deal."

"Is that what they did that first time?" The quiet clickety-clack of the keyboard fell silent.

"Goodwin's doesn't sell all the kinds of stuff it used to back then. We're using what we can—small appliances, household goods, some of their Christmas home décor that fits the tone." She gestured weakly.

"Nothing like the good old days, huh? That store used to have a little of everything. In fact, it used to take up most of the block."

"They still own the building next door and

keep all the utilities on in it. They use it as a warehouse for the current stock, sale stuff and, well, other stuff." She thought about sharing her conclusion that Doc hung on to the multistoried building chock-full of old merchandise, mannequins and countless display materials because it represented his reluctance to let go of the past.

"Interesting," Bivvy droned, clearly not interested at all. "The lights are about to go off in one…two…three."

Everything outside went dark and quiet.

Addie heaved a sigh of relief.

"Now to check the comments left by people from all over the world."

"Really? People all over the world are looking at our little house in Star City, Tennessee?"

"You give people something interesting to look at, something out of the ordinary, something sentimental, something with a little style and they will just naturally be drawn to it. I've got so many fans and followers this year I decided to join in a contest."

That made Addie nervous. "What kind of contest?"

"I'm trying to get the most votes as the best Christmas house. If I get picked, I get a flash to put on my Web site for next year and maybe a nearby TV news crew or one of those home and garden–type shows will come out and film my display."

"Mom." Addie shook her head. "Why would you even want that?"

"Because that's what I *do*, Adelaide, sweetie." Bivvy pushed back her chair and stood. Her features were softened by love and good humor as she came down the hall and put her hands on either side of her daughter's face. "When I believe in something, I don't care who knows it. And I believe in Christmas. I believe in shining a light on the love of God brought to us through the gift of Jesus. When people come to my Web site, they see that story. When they look at our home or at me, they see that joy."

Addie nodded. "You've given me a lot to think about, Mom."

Addie arrived at work to find that none of the people she had contacted about publicity for the promotion seemed interested in covering it. The only one she hadn't heard from was the local paper, the *Star City Satellite.*

She called, and someone there promised

to call her back. She thought about what her mom had told her about attracting attention, about giving people something out of the ordinary, stylish and sentimental. That had given her an idea.

"Hey! Maimie said I might find you over here." Nate caught up with her by the elevator on the third floor offices that led to the unused warehouse side of the store.

She had seen Nate every day for the last seven days straight, but they hadn't been alone a minute of it. Maimie had always been there going over details, asking questions. Or Doc, telling stories. Or Jesse, just being Jesse.

"And here I am." She reached for the elevator button.

He did the same, his hand coming down on top of hers.

She jerked away, embarrassed at the flinching quickness of her reaction. She cleared her throat and pressed the button several more times, as if that would make the elevator arrive faster.

"Did you need me for something?" she asked, her voice wavering slightly.

"Nope." He stood back and folded his arms over his pale blue shirt with a sword-fish motif. The outfit only served to remind her that he would rather be anywhere but here. "Now that they've enrolled Jesse in a private Christian school, I have some time on my hands during school hours. I just wanted to see if I could help you out."

"Thanks." She tugged her gray cardigan closed over her turtleneck and navy blue wool pants. "I've always been one of those 'the more, the merrier' types."

He smiled. "I don't know how merry we'll be, but I'm happy to help."

The elevator dinged to signal its arrival. For a split second Addie had second thoughts about walking into such close quarters with this man. The doors rattled open.

"Happy is good," she said softly as she turned her shoulders in order to slip easily past him. "So is help."

He got in.

She took a deep breath and tried to act casual, as if she had not spent the last few days watching him, wondering how things might be different if he weren't on his way out of Star City on December twenty-fourth and she weren't going to stay here as long as she possibly could.

Of course, that hinged on her being able to bring Goodwin's back from the brink.

As the door slid shut on the upper floor of the warehouse building, she said, "I thought we should go through the old Christmas displays. Doc says they're scattered all around this building, but the oldest ones should be on the first floor, near what used to be the second set of windows."

"Cool." He faced forward.

She thought about making small talk, about asking him how Jesse liked the new school or when Darin Goodwin was expected to return from his honeymoon. But Doc had told her that Jesse loved the school and Darin would be back in a few days at least twice already.

Just keep your mouth shut and your mind on the task at hand, she told herself. Then she stole a sideways peek at Nate.

She thought of how great he was with Jesse, how patient and kind. And how, with just a few words or a wink, he could have stern Maimie Goodwin giggling like a schoolgirl. She thought of how it had felt to throw convention to the wind and kiss him the first day she'd ever laid eyes on him.

That thought made her cheeks burn hot and her throat close up, but not so much that she didn't manage to blurt something out in hopes of distracting him, and herself, from her discomfort. "So, if I can't get any publicity for this publicity stunt, what do you think the Goodwins will do?"

"You'll get the publicity." He sounded so sure.

She wanted to believe him. The elevator dinged to say it had settled on the second floor, and the doors shambled open on a floor packed full of furniture, probably display models from over the years, and stacks of old household goods still in their boxes.

"Is this an elevator or a time machine?" Nate wondered aloud.

"I wish it were a time machine. I'd love to have seen this old store in its heyday. I don't recall it as much different from the way it is today." She sighed and pushed the button for the first floor.

As the doors slid shut again, Nate looked at her with a kind but curious gaze. "You really do love this place, don't you?"

"Every bit as much or more than you want to get away from it," she shot back, not meeting his eyes for fear he might see how sad the reminders made her of what Goodwin's had once been and what he and she could never be.

"I don't want to get away from it," he corrected her with a gentle power in his hushed tone.

"You don't?" Her hair fell over her shoulder as she swung her head to make eye contact with him at last.

"I just don't have any particular reason to stay." His gaze did not waver as he added, quietly, "Unless…"

The elevator dinged once again, and this time the door rolled open smoothly.

"Unless what?" she wanted to scream but kept silent instead.

"Guess this is our floor," he said, extending his arm to encourage her to move ahead of him. "What are you looking for?"

She gazed up into his eyes.

"I'm looking for something that I'm not sure I'll ever find," she whispered enigmatically before she squared her shoulders and got back to work. "That is, anything that might date back to the original publicity stunt. Doc says they used the same signage for the first four years, so they had lots of duplicates."

She marched to the light switches and flipped them on. Bright light flooded the whole floor—not that they could easily have found anything light or no light.

"Doc Goodwin does not want to close this store." In an instant Nate summed up what Addie had suspected since she saw all the stuff stored in this building.

She forged ahead, working her way through the stacks of boxes and store counters and display units still positioned where they had been placed many years ago. "Unfortunately, I don't think his son wants to take responsibility for it."

"Or anything," Nate muttered as he followed close behind her.

"You're worried about Jesse." She had almost reached the front of the store. She began to work her way toward a stash of tall, flat cardboard boxes marked Christmas and Goodlife that were propped against the brown paper covering the front window.

"He's a great kid who hasn't gotten a lot of great breaks in life." Nate reached the boxes, and seeming to know she wanted to get a peek inside them, he began moving away the things hemming them in. "I wish I could do more for him. Even the school they have him in is struggling."

"I know. My church sponsors it. I recommended it to the Goodwins because I knew there were so many good people trying to make it work." She, too, began to move objects, starting with a stack of plastic chairs, which she had to remove one by one. "But enrollment is down, and some of the teachers and administrators are talking about having to find other jobs."

"The place I'm interviewing in L.A. has so much money coming in, and yet apparently they are always holding fundraisers and raking in more." He paused with the last box still in his hands and asked, "You don't think we can talk Maimie into putting a donation box up in the store, do you?"

Before Addie could comment on that, she had set aside the last chair and turned to find him freeing the tall box.

"What exactly are we looking for here?" he asked.

"I'm not too picky. I've already seen some items I think we can haul over to set the fifties mood in the windows. But I'd love to find promo items with that classic retro style or—"

"Or the biggest relic of all, a happy nuclear family?"

She twisted in the spot where she stood and looked at all the stuff around them and laughed. "I wouldn't be surprised if there was an actual family living in all this, totally untouched by time."

"Well, it's not an actual family, but say hello to our counterparts." He came to her side, plopped his arm around her shoulder and turned her toward the box he had just opened.

There stood a life-sized photographic cardboard cutout of a mom, dad, kid and dog frozen in time circa 1959. The father wore a green sweater over a white shirt and rust-colored tie. The mother had her requisite high heels and pearls, naturally, but she also had a perfect figure and wore a holiday hostess apron over her perfectly fitting dress.

"The little boy could be Jesse," Nate observed. "Or Opie from *The Andy Griffith Show*."

"No, definitely Jesse," Addie said as the image tugged at her heartstrings. She was finding it hard to catch her breath standing there and with Nate's arm around her staring at the family she and Nate were expected to portray. "We aren't really the spitting images of the couple, though, huh?"

"It's not exactly like looking in a mirror." He laughed, then let go of her. "Or like looking at any family Christmas I have ever been a part of."

"We always had a big celebration at Christmas," she said. "Even the year my dad was dying."

He stopped midreach in his efforts to get the sign free and looked at her. "I'm sorry. I didn't know."

"It's okay. I was young, but my mom and dad handled it so well. I was sad, and I miss him to this day, but I also got a chance to see real faith in action." Her eyes grew moist, but she did not cry.

He listened intently.

"Dad was so brave, right up until the end. Since then my mom has always…" Addie stopped to think of her mom and their discussion this morning. She could practically hear the hum of all the lights and motors from their front-lawn display as she fought back a wave of embarrassment at how hard she had always been about her mother's Christmas antics and said, "She always made a point to celebrate big at Christmas after that."

"So you doing this promo is probably making her very happy?"

In that moment she felt at least a little comforted about her years of trying to distance herself from her mom's displays. "Yes, I guess, it—"

"Addie McCoy, phone call on line one." The voice of the lady from the customer-service counter echoed through the building.

"I better take that. It might be the *Star City Satellite*." She excused herself and hurried to the phone attached to a column behind an empty sales counter.

Moments later she found herself listening to the editor of the *Satellite* telling her he didn't see any value in doing a story on Goodwin's Christmas promotion. "It's just not newsworthy. If they want to pay for an ad, I'd be happy to talk."

Addie stiffened. Everything she had worked so hard to achieve these last few days came down to this. Goodwin's needed publicity. She was in charge of marketing, and if this editor hung up now, she would have failed to get any advance word out. She wasn't sure what to do. Her gaze fell on the cardboard cutout, then on Nate. She thought of what he had said about Jesse and his school, then about her mom loving all this. She recalled what she had learned about the Web cam, the contest and how to give people what they wanted.

There was also the idea that something could compel Nate to perhaps want to stay in Star City, but not if he left because the promotion got cancelled.

"All right, you want newsworthy?" She took a deep breath and gripped the phone receiver tightly. "How about this? In a matter of days, Goodwin's Department Store is going to go back in time and around the world. We are going to give people something to feel sentimental about, something to cheer for and something to help them show their commitment to Christmas and help children in the process. If that's newsworthy enough for you, show up here Thursday morning and bring your camera."

Chapter Six

If anyone at the temp agency would have warned him when he took this assignment that there was even the slightest chance that twelve days before Christmas he'd be still in Star City, dressed like a dad straight out of a 1950s family sitcom, Nate would have turned the job down cold.

But if he hadn't taken the job caring for Jesse Goodwin, he'd have missed out on so much. First and foremost, of course, getting to know a great kid and being able to make a difference in his life, however fleeting. Next, he'd have missed meeting all the great people of Star City, from the Goodwins to the parents and teachers at Jesse's school to Addie McCoy.

He stood back and folded his arms over

his gray suit jacket, courtesy of the costume department of the Star City Community Theater, to watch his counterpart at work. Somehow in the last five days she had managed to take the Christmas promotion in hand and spin it off in a whole new direction. With Web cams streaming live directly from inside Goodwin's on a Web site set to go live in a matter of minutes, she'd already garnered attention from all over. It helped that she had found a way to connect the whole stunt to a worthy cause—raising money for Jesse's school—and to get people engaged by turning the whole thing into a competition.

He took a leisurely stroll the length of the windows. At the far ends of each, Addie had hung signs that read His and Hers. Each side had been furnished with the trappings people associated with the life and times of a husband or wife circa 1959. "His" featured a desk and office furnishings. "Hers" had a kitchen complete with a sink, stove, fridge—a set also courtesy of the community theater—and a chrome-and-Formica table she'd brought from her own home. In a stroke of what he considered genius on Addie's part, she had also arranged a sofa, an old television, a faux fireplace and a spot to set up a Christmas tree in the entryway just inside the store. It was a place that could be viewed from the door or, if you craned your neck just so, from the windows but was best seen by coming into Goodwin's.

And that's just what people were doing. Sales were up, though not breaking any records, but Maimie reported that foot traffic had almost doubled, and now that the promotion was going into full swing they expected that to grow considerably. Anyone looking at the goings-on today would think that the Goodwins themselves were responsible for all this. They were the ones front and center, and Maimie was going to be the one presenting everything at the launch and in any subsequent media contacts.

All of this made Nate smile. In part because he had believed Addie capable of all of this from the moment she rallied her nerve and kissed him that morning under the mistletoe. But he also couldn't keep from celebrating privately because he knew that Addie had gotten what she wanted: success for Goodwin's and a meaningful job behind the scenes and as part of a team.

He turned away from the small but energetic crowd gathering outside the still-closed doors of the old department store in time to see Addie walking toward him.

"Well, if it isn't the little woman," he said, smiling so big his cheeks hurt as she walked up to him in those simple heels she'd worn the day they met and one of the dresses she had found at a vintage-clothing store over in Gatlinburg. "I have to say, it looks good on you."

"This old thing?" She swished the full, gathered skirt one way then another, giving a half turn, then dipping her chin and batting her eyes just like a starlet straight out of the 1950s.

"Not the outfit," he said, coming to her side so that they could present a united front when the store doors opened. "All of this." He extended his arm to indicate everything surrounding them. "The enthusiasm of the public, the appreciation of the Goodwins, the cooperation of the press. Success. *Success* looks good on you, Addie."

"Thank you, Nate." She practically beamed like a lighted angel on the top of a Christmas tree, but one quick look at him top to toes and it was like somebody pulled the plug. "You don't really look all that different."

"I tucked my hair behind my ears," he

protested, though not convincingly because she hadn't told him anything he hadn't already thought himself.

"Oh, it's okay. Don't worry about it." She gave his arm a pat. "It will give me an instant edge in the voting for who is making the transition to life in the fifties better."

He hadn't thought of that. Even though all the money collected would end up benefiting Jesse's school, Nate had just enough of a competitive nature to want plenty of that money to have come from his supporters. If he had to go old school—literally—to accomplish that? He opened his mouth to tell her not to get too comfy in that assumption, but just then Maimie and Doc stepped up to the front door.

Addie fluffed her hair, smoothed down her skirt, squared her shoulders, wet her lips and through a perfect smile said, "Showtime!"

"Ladies and gentlemen." Maimie raised her hands, commanding all eyes outside and in. "Welcome to Goodwin's Department Store. Home for the next twelve days, excluding Sundays, of course, of Nathan and Adelaide Goodlife."

As the small group applauded politely, Nate turned to his counterpart and whispered,

"You know I've been so involved in taking care of Jesse and pitching in around here when I can, I never thought about the actual event. What are we going to do all day long?"

Outside Maimie raised her hands again, and the group, which had drifted from applause to foot-shuffling and mumbling, quieted.

Addie froze. "I've been so focused on the Web stuff and getting the word out that when Maimie said she'd take care of all of that, I left it to her."

Nate's stomach lurched as if it had actually taken a dive from the height of his admiration for Addie to the depths of his good-natured frustration in dealing with the formidable Mrs. Goodwin.

"The Goodlifes will be going through these next few days demonstrating life as we knew it way back when Goodwin's first opened its doors, fifty years ago."

He adjusted his tie, which suddenly felt much tighter around his throat than before, and muttered, "I have a bad feeling about this."

Chapter Seven

Christmas with Mr. and Mrs. Goodlife
See how good the Goodwin's life can be
10 a.m.—7 p.m. Monday-Wednesday
10 a.m.—8 p.m. Thursday-Saturday
Closed Sundays

Addie stared at the sign posted front and center in her side of the twin plate-glass windows. Because the whole stunt had morphed into a challenge for charity, she and Nate had agreed to longer than normal hours six days a week. In return they got time off to enjoy hot lunches brought in by local eateries, to take breaks to roam the store and talk with customers, even run errands around town as long as they stayed in character and costume. Though they never got to leave the windows at the same time.

In accordance with Maimie's agenda, Addie gave three cooking demos a day, though since the oven wasn't functional she didn't actually cook so much as combine ingredients, put them in the oven and then take a break to "wash up," run to the break-room and pick up a premade clone of what she had made. Sometimes it worked all right, but for the most part Mrs. Goodlife came off looking like a pretty lame home-maker. The crafts projects went better, to some degree, but because she had to stick with ideas gathered from women's maga-zines of the day, they tended to be heavy in the glitter and spray-painted macaroni depart-ment.

She sank into the unforgiving stiffness of the kitchen chair.

"How's life on the home front, Mrs. Goodlife?" Nate called out from his side of the dual display.

"Boring," she called back, unafraid to speak frankly in the midafternoon lull with no customers around to hear her.

"What do you expect? It's 1959. Fun hasn't been invented yet," he teased.

She laughed, then sighed. "I had no idea it would be this tedious."

"Tedious? You want to talk tedious? Try sitting at a desk all day pretending to shuffle paperwork when what you're really doing is monitoring the Web site, posting blog updates and reading through the comments, a third of which wouldn't make sense even if they were spelled right."

"You find that tedious?" She slapped her palms flat on the tabletop then pushed back her chair and stood. She walked toward the side of her window nearest to him, stretching up on tiptoe as if that might help carry her voice as she called out, "Are you kidding? I'd love that. I'm stuck over here in the kitchen all day doing demos every ninety minutes. In a day and a half I've done more cooking and crafting here than I did the whole year and a half since I graduated from college."

"Year and a half, huh? So that makes you…"

"Twenty-four. I'm twenty-four years old, still live at home and this was supposed to be my first real grown-up job that has anything to do with my marketing major. Only for this job I'd have done better with

a home ec major." She blurted out the whole
frustrating truth.

"…three years younger than me," Nate
concluded. "I was going to say you're three
years younger than me, but the rest of that
was interesting, too. Thanks for sharing."

"I'm sorry. I'm just a little jumpy, I
guess." She slumped her shoulders forward
and laughed at that. "I blame all this glitter
and gelatin."

She walked to the faux cabinets and picked
up a box with the brand name hidden behind
a phony label. Since they were live streaming
over the Web, the Goodwin's attorney had felt
more comfortable if they kept all references
to products not sold in the store obscured and
referred to them only by generic terms.

"At least you have some human contact,"
Nate grumbled—if you could call something as loud as that a grumble, she thought.

She looked up at the large clock above the
stairway at the back of the store and realized
she needed to get ready for her next demo.
As she began gathering things on the countertop, she reminded Nate, "At least at three
o'clock *you* get to put up a sign saying you're
in a business meeting and dash out and pick
up Jesse from school every afternoon."

Darin Goodwin had been home from his honeymoon for days now, but beyond giving Jesse a place to sleep at night he had done nothing to try to bond with the child. Maimie and Doc fussed and fretted about that, making excuses for their son's behavior and assuring everyone who asked about the situation that it would all work out, probably after Christmas.

Addie looked at the cardboard cutout of the happy family complete with the little boy who looked a little like Jesse and then at the makings for a Popsicle-stick manger craft project in her hands. Picking up the cutout of the star she would later cover in macaroni and spray paint gold, she walked slowly past the living-room set, past the front door of the store and leaned one shoulder against the wall of Nate's set. "What do you think will happen to Jesse when you leave?"

He looked up at her and gave a sort of sad smile, then shook his head as he said softly, "You're not supposed to be over here during office hours, Mrs. Goodlife."

"Maybe I had to come, Mr. Goodlife. Maybe you forgot something when you hurried out the door for work this morning."

"What?" He pushed up from the office chair where he spent so much of his day pretending to do paperwork and came her way. "My goodbye kiss, I hope."

"No!" Heat rose from her roll-collar neckline to her cheeks, and she tipped her head down, hoping that he wouldn't see her blush. "I, uh, I…" She slipped her hand into her apron pocket, found the box of gelatin and pulled it free. "I brought you lunch."

He leaned in close.

Her stomach fluttered. She watched him move closer, thinking she should tell him that some kids from the school would be by any minute on a field trip and the last thing they wanted was to get caught kissing. She pressed her lips together.

His face came so close to hers she could see his cheek twitch with amusement as he snatched the box from her hand and said, "Yum-yum."

He pulled away, and she let her breath out in a long stream. Then she came to her senses, reached out and nabbed the box back again. "Sorry. I need that for a demo later."

With that she turned on her high heel to start back to her kitchen set. Outside, the sound of an engine drew her attention as a big yellow school bus pulled to the curb. "Time to get back to work, Mr. Goodlife."

"Why do I suddenly have great empathy for zoo animals?" he muttered as he made a quick pass—straightening his tie and jacket and making sure his too-shaggy-for-the-time-period hair was tucked behind his ears.

"You just have to look good. I have ten minutes to construct a manger, then show them how to make a gelatin fruit salad in a mold." She held up the star and the box on either side of her head as though doing an advertisement for them both. "I just hope I don't get my gelatin and my glitter mixed up!"

She scooted across the way, still a bit breathless over the near-miss chance for a kiss. As she passed the door, it flung open and in came a class of kids that looked a year or so older than Jesse. With teachers and moms keeping them in line, they came inside single file, but as soon as they saw Nate and Addie they scattered. Even though they had all joked about the archaic roles of men and women, Addie couldn't help noting that the boys rushed over to check out Nate's area while the girls clustered in the cozy little kitchen setting.

"Hey, who are you supposed to be,

mister?" one of the boys who wriggled his way to the front of the group demanded loudly of Nate.

"I'm Mr. Goodlife."

Silence and befuddled expressions answered that.

He tried again. "The…dad?"

"Oh, I get it," another boy called out. "You and that mom are divorced, so you have to live over here and the mom lives over there."

The matter-of-factness with which the boy spouted that conclusion tugged at Addie's heart. She held her hand up to ask the gaggle of girls around the table to wait a moment, and she started to go over to Nate's side to see if she could help out.

Of course Nate, with his master's in child development and a matter of weeks as a manny under his belt, didn't need help.

"I'm supposed to be at the office," he confided, trying to look quite businesslike.

The boys looked at each other.

"Work," he clarified.

"You sure do dress funny for work," another boy observed, shaking his head in a show of obvious disbelief.

"This is how they dressed for work back then. This is how they dressed for church and for going out to eat and even, some-times, for doing everyday things like going to a movie or ball game."

"No way!" They stared at him, their mouths gaping. "Every day?"

"Yep. Every day." He moved from the office toward the living-room set in the middle ground between the two windows. The boys followed, and seeing the action, the girls moved forward to get a good look. "And when a man came home from work, he would take off his jacket and tie and put on a sweater or a more casual jacket. They tried to look nice even if they were just watching TV."

Nate sat on the couch, looking every bit the man of that era as king of his castle.

"Dads even dressed up when they came home?" One of the girls ventured forward. "What about when they ran the vacuum or helped their kids do stuff? Kids were still messy back then, right?"

He laughed. "I'm sure they were, but the way I understand it, most dads didn't do housework back then or help raising the kids."

"What *did* they do?" The first boy who spoke up wanted to know.

Nate looked at Addie for help.

She folded her arms to let him know he was on his own.

"Well, they had some household chores, sure. But after a hard day as family bread-winner they usually came home and read the newspaper, maybe watched TV until their dinner was ready."

"Wow. No wonder the mommy makes you live in your office!" a small but feisty girl standing by Addie exclaimed. "You don't do nothin'!"

The adults laughed.

Nate looked a bit sheepish.

Addie stepped up to chime in, "You know that we're just playing roles here. In the real world, Nate is actually a professional child-care provider and all-around great husband." Addie's cheeks blazed red the second she realized what she had called him.

"Guy," she corrected hastily. "All-around great guy."

Their eyes met. He smiled but did not have anything to add. Not that she would have heard it with her now-slowing heart-beat thudding in her ears.

"He still doesn't look like that guy." The first boy to raise the issue went to the card-board cutout and pointed to the perpetually cheerful father figure towering over the family portrait.

"You know, you're right!" Maimie Goodwin with her hands folded in front of her strolled elegantly into the fray. She stopped beside the sign and gave it a good looking over before she tipped her nose up and studied Nate. "He doesn't quite look the part, does he?"

"Oh, no, Maimie." Nate put his hand up. A lesser man might have retreated a step or two from the formidable older woman, but Nate held his ground. "Don't get any ideas in your head."

"I assure you, *Mr. Goodlife*—" she emphasized the name with her imperious tone and threw in an arched eyebrow for good measure just to make sure he and anyone else who might be drawing a paycheck with her signature on it got the message loud and clear "—I always have ideas. Goodwin's Department Store opened in 1959 and is still here today because I got some ideas in my head."

"Let me guess, you're getting a new idea right now?" He folded his arms and cocked his head in an "if you can't beat 'em, join 'em" kind of conspiratory way. "One that involves me and the missus?"

"Actually, it just involved you, Mr. Goodlife, but now that you mention it…" She turned her smile to Addie. It was a gentle smile, but the set of her cheeks and the narrowing of her eyes made it clear she wasn't joking when she said, "I seem to recall that *some* women found being a housewife in 1959 could be quite… What was the word I heard bandied about?"

She fixed that arched eyebrow on Addie.

"Tedious?" Addie offered in a whisper, knowing she'd been caught.

Maimie's smile warmed considerably, and she looked down at the children staring up at her and the sign showing the perfect Goodwin's family as she told them, "Tomorrow being Saturday, children, tell your parents to come down to Goodwin's first thing. There are going to be some exciting changes taking place, and I have an *idea* you are all going to love them."

Chapter Eight

The next day Addie arrived dressed in black pencil-thin slacks and a pale blue angora sweater to find her way to the front door of Goodwin's blocked by a media circus—or what passed for a media circus in Star City. There was even a van with Mountain Aspect Productions painted on the side. Addie stood on the sidewalk and stared at the seemingly endless stream of young men and women emerging from that van carrying cameras, cords and sound and computer equipment into the store.

The little bit of breakfast Addie had managed to choke down this morning practically soured in her stomach at all the excitement, knowing she hadn't generated any of it. For weeks she had called and sent press releases and done all that Web work, and nobody had shown up. Maimie Goodwin told a few kids to tell their parents, and what happened? Of course she knew that Maimie had done more than make a passing remark to the kids yesterday. In fact, she had been a very busy woman.

The instant she saw the top of an elegantly styled silver hairdo, Addie knew she had to confront the woman or admit she couldn't do the job. "Mrs. Goodwin, can I have a word with you about all this... this..."

"It's digital, dear. Or hi-def? Oh, I don't really know what it's called, exactly." She waved off her confusion, then pointed toward the stairway to direct a young man with a camera on his shoulder that way. "The upshot is, we're making a commercial!"

"A commercial?" Addie followed along a few steps behind the older woman, suddenly feeling as though she would never fully catch up. "When I suggested a commercial early on, you said it wasn't necessary. I wish you'd have let me know that you changed your mind. I would have—"

"Don't worry, dear. You don't have to do a thing. Doc and I are just going to invite people to see how good the Goodwin's life can be. It's only a thirty-second spot."

"But as the one in charge of marketing for—"

"Once again, Addie, not to worry." Maimie held her hand up. "You will have plenty to do when the Web experts get here."

That made her pull up short. "Web experts?"

"Oh, yes. Your Web site and everything you've done on the Internet has opened our eyes to all the opportunities we've missed by not having an online presence." Maimie kept breezing right on through the store, leaving Addie behind.

"Online presence?" she murmured, trying to figure out how this whole project had gotten so out of her control and how she, who had proposed it in an effort to create a long-term job for herself, had gotten lost in it all. She started walking after Mrs. Goodwin again, raising her voice to ask, "You…you replaced me?"

"Not so much replaced you as hired someone to do the work you might have done if you weren't already busy playing Mrs. Goodlife." She stopped, looked around, spotted Doc and waved to him. Then, when he started in her direction, she hurried off to meet him, calling behind her, "I know we can't really get much done by Christmas, but we're thinking of having a few specialty items up for people to order, our commercial, a link to your Web cam and pages."

"But I'm the one who is supposed to do all this, to coordinate and come up with marketing plans and…" And no one was listening to her.

Except Nate, who came up behind her, standing so close that his casual collegiate cardigan rasped against the fuzzy knit of her sweater when he folded his arms and said, "Now you know how I felt that day I said I'd postpone my trip back home a few days to take care of Jesse and ended up as—"

"My holiday husband," she whispered. "I don't suppose you have any clue what she has planned for us today?"

"Big plans! Oh, she has big plans for today," Doc said as he hustled past. "Big announcement!"

Addie shut her eyes. "All of this should have come through me. I thought this was my job."

"It is your job. Go fight for it." Nate had leaned in so close, she could feel his breath against her ear.

She resisted the urge to shiver by concentrating on what the man had said, not how he had said it or where he was standing when he said it. She lifted her chin, trying to convince herself more than him as she said, "Me? Stand up to Maimie Goodwin? You really think that's going to work?"

He laughed. "She hired you because you brought her something she believed in."

"The publicty stunt."

"You," he corrected. "Addie McCoy. That hasn't changed. You are still as valuable to her as you were a couple of weeks ago. More so, actually, because you've contributed plenty to this business since then and, unless I miss my guess, learned plenty."

"You know, I have."

"It wouldn't do any harm to remind her of that. It also wouldn't hurt your cause if you have a solid concept to offer her."

"I do! Webisodes!" She clutched his arm, barely able to keep her excitement in check. "My mom's Web site is up all night long, but then during the day she runs little 'How to Deck the Halls' videos she's done so she still gets hits. I had this idea that we could do a few short pieces that are actually advertisements for Goodwin's where Mrs. Goodlife has a dream that she is transported to the future and sees that even fifty years from now a Goodwin's life is still the good life!"

"That's great. Way to use your head, Mrs. Goodlife." He tapped her black velveteen headband, making her cherished snowflake pin, which she had attached to the band to keep from making a hole in her vintage sweater, bobble. "Did I knock your snowflake loose?"

She reached up to test it. "No, it's fine. I always make sure it's pretty secure. I wouldn't want to lose it for the world. It was a gift from my father that last Christmas."

"Ah. I knew there was a story behind it."

"When he gave it to me, my dad said that since he couldn't always be with me, it was his way to remind me that I was a special and unique individual, that there was nobody out there just like me."

"Like a snowflake."

"Exactly. But he also wanted me to remember that even though every snowflake is beautiful on its own, many of them working together can totally change the way people see their whole world."

"I like that."

She met his warm, sincere gaze. "Of

course, my mom really played up the 'beauty of the individual' angle."

"And you liked the 'everyone working together' bit?"

"Yeah. That is, I did, but now…" She looked toward Mrs. Goodwin, who had finally gotten the production team sent off to prepare for their commercial and was now talking to Doc in the living-room setting, probably going over last-minute details of her big announcement.

"To everything there is a season," Nate said quietly, clearly reading a pending shift of her feelings in her wistful hesitation. "And a time to every purpose under the heavens."

Addie skimmed her fingers over the snow-flake again. Even with all the chaos around them she had a sense of the whole world being no bigger than the space where she and Nate now stood. "I love that part of Ecclesiastes."

He adjusted his vintage harvest-gold V-neck sweater over his broad shoulders. "Just a little something to think about."

"At one point in your life it's good to work together with others, and at other times you just have to work up your nerve and…" She gestured with both hands as she tried to find the right way to put it.

"Be a flake?" he quipped.

She smiled. "I was going to say to go out there and stand out."

"Even better." He put his hands on her shoulders, fixed his eyes on hers and then, just before he let go, leaned down and gave her a quick kiss on the cheek. "Go. Let Maimie know that Mrs. Goodlife isn't the only one with her sights on the future."

She didn't think her feet touched the ground after that kiss and Nate's show of faith in her. She floated along to the living-room set, imagined herself practically hovering as she shared her proposal for the webisodes and drifted even higher emotionally when the older woman told her she thought they were brilliant.

When Nate came to her side to hear the big announcement, she wondered if, in the still photos being snapped by the photographer of the *Star City Satellite*, it would show she was over the moon. Or if, minutes later, when Mrs. Goodwin took the floor to command the attention of the group, everyone standing there noticed that before the older woman finished her exciting proclamation, Addie wished she could crawl in a hole and hide.

Chapter Nine

Nate had to remind himself to keep smiling as Maimie launched into a spiel welcoming the curious and the customers and singing the praises of Goodwin's Department Store. Though smiling wasn't so difficult when he glanced at Addie standing to his right.

"Psst." She jerked her head slightly to the side and shifted her eyes to get his attention and ask him to get close enough to hear her. When he obliged, she whispered, "No matter what she says…"

"I know, keep smiling."

"Stay cool," she finished for him.

"I am cool." He didn't even sound convincing to himself.

"You are so jumpy you have been finishing my sentences all day." She looked up at him from the corners of her eyes. "And getting them wrong."

He cleared his throat and tugged at his sweater collar, then pushed back his hair.

"So just follow my lead. I had to agree to a little something with Mrs. Goodwin in order to get her to stop talking and listen to me."

"Just what did you agree to? Where am I following your lead to?"

She raised her finger to her lips as if to shush him and whispered, "Cool."

"You got it. I'm as cool as you, my little snowflake," he muttered. Then, catching what he had said, he held out his hand in a 'hold it right there' kind of gesture and said distinctly, "Not that you're *mine*. I'm not trying to stake a claim on you."

The gathering crowd fell silent, and he realized that Mrs. Goodwin had just finished speaking and everyone had heard him tell Addie she was not his.

She squirmed.

He fell back on the old reliable smile. It had no impact on Maimie, who gave him a shake of her head before she turned back to the group, held up her hands and said, "And now for our big announcement. There are going to be some big changes for our promotional couple, the Goodlifes."

Nate looked at Addie, who stared straight ahead.

"In response to those who rightfully pointed out that our gentleman's work life is decidedly un-fifties-like in comparison to our lady's, starting Monday, Mr. Goodlife will have a secretary."

He looked to Addie, but her wide eyes were fixed on a woman in a towering beehive hairdo with a pencil stuck in it, cat eye glasses and an orange tweed suit.

"Mom!"

Bivvy McCoy wiggle-walked her way onto the scene to the delight of the entire store full of people. "Ain't it a hoot, Addie-baby? When I told 'em this was for charity, I got time off from work to come by a couple times a day."

Addie's face went nearly white.

"Cool," Nate murmured in Addie's ear, then added, "I take it this is not the little something you agreed to?"

The answer came not from Addie but from Maimie, who thanked Bivvy with a poised head nod, then commanded everyone's attention again by saying, "And Mr. Goodlife is not the only one with big changes in store."

All eyes moved to Addie, and she tensed.

He put his hand on her shoulder and stepped up close behind her. "It's all for charity. Plus, the end result will get you what you've always wanted."

"Mrs. Goodlife is going to become a mother!"

Nate curved his fingers around Addie's upper arm and got a good grip, fearing she might faint. Of course, she didn't faint. Addie was made of stronger stuff than that. *Keep cool,* he reminded himself as he grinned and, trying to take the attention off Addie, said, "I guess that means I'm going to be a dad."

The crowd broke into wild applause.

Addie shot him a panicked look. "Nate! How could you?"

Nate tried to quiet the group, but Maimie took things in hand when she laughed and explained. "Our grandson, Jesse, will be filling in as Jesse Goodlife a few hours a day while on Christmas break from school."

"Jesse." Addie relaxed and whispered, "Oh, that's so perfect."

This time he didn't have to remind himself

to smile. The way Addie had taken to Jesse got to him on a gut level. He'd always been a kid person. He had taken enough courses in psychology to know that stemmed from his own feelings of vulnerability and loneliness in childhood. He also knew that identifying it wouldn't change who he was or lessen the way he felt when he saw how open and loving Addie was to this kid who needed a little kindness and warmth in his life.

"Finally, I want to issue an invitation." Maimie launched into her concluding remarks.

Addie's spine went rigid. She whipped her head around and angled her shoulders back so that she could say, unnoticed by those around them, "This is it. Don't panic. I know just what to do."

In Nate's experience a sentence like that never led to anything good.

"Next Saturday the Goodlifes are holding a Christmas Open House."

Addie cocked her head, and Nate figured that wasn't what she had expected to hear. Once again Maimie had gone off on her own, he guessed, leaving Addie feeling foolish and frustrated.

"Please feel free to drop by anytime, all day. There will be door prizes, and everyone who comes in 1950s-style costume will be entered in a drawing for a grand prize. I hope to see you all there."

"Whew. Got through the whole thing and not even a hint of panic," he teased her.

"She's got so much going she even glosses over her own ideas." She folded her arms. "How can I ever expect her to listen to me and take me seriously?"

"Oh, I almost forgot." Maimie turned back toward the group for just a moment. "One last change that involves our couple that you all might find interesting." She looked right at Addie, winked, then nailed Nate with a steely glare. "Mr. Goodlife is going to get a haircut."

"A what?" Nate asked.

The crowd applauded again.

"And Mrs. Goodlife is the one who is going to give it to him," Maimie added. "Ten minutes from now, front of the store. Have a good day!"

"Mrs. Goodlife? Front of the store?" No wonder Addie had told him to stay cool. She knew this was just the kind of thing that would get him hot under the collar. He turned to her.

"Trust me," she pleaded before he could get his protest out.

He hadn't planned on getting his hair cut until his job interview. But then he hadn't planned any of this so far, and he'd been having a pretty good time. A much better time than he'd have had alone in L.A., he realized, looking into Addie's sweet face as her expression told him how much this meant to her and the future she had always dreamed of. "I didn't plan on getting my hair cut until someone as lovely as Mrs. Goodlife could do it for me."

She smiled and mouthed a silent thank-you.

He offered her his arm. "My display case or yours?"

With a good many of the people who had stopped to listen to Maimie's announcements watching, Nate took a seat at the kitchen table and awaited his fate.

"This won't hurt a bit," Addie teased as she pulled a green and pink and white 1950s-style Christmas tablecloth from a drawer.

He clenched his jaw and tried not to sound too concerned as he asked, "You *do* have some experience giving haircuts, don't you, dear?"

"Of course I do, darling." She gave the tablecloth a flick, and it unfurled with a pop.

As she began to drape it around his upper body like a barber's cape, she mugged to the crowd and said, "I've been practicing on the neighbor's poodle!"

The crowd laughed.

He started to get up out of the chair, but she pushed him down again, and as she tied the tablecloth around his neck, she nonchalantly put her lips near his ear and whispered, "I've got this all figured out. I'll cut some of the curly part that hangs over your ears and collar, then slick it back with water so it looks fifties-ish."

"If you use water on my hair, when it dries it will be even curlier," he warned.

"Then I'll use something else I have in the kitchen. How about shortening?" She gave his shoulder a pat, then made a show of going to the drawers again, saying things like, "Now where are my kitchen shears? I don't want to use my good sewing scissors for a messy job like this."

"Messy?" He sat up and gave the crowd a worried look that was not far from how he felt. "Maybe I ought to go to a real barber, dear."

"Nonsense. I can do this. You do have faith in me, don't you, Nathan?" She stood over him, kitchen shears in hand. She snipped them in the air a few times and raised her eyebrows, trying to look sinister.

He chuckled softly at the attempt but not at the question. "Adelaide, my dear, I have more faith in you than I have had in anyone in a long time."

And he meant it.

She knew he meant it, too, because all the playfulness of her pretense fell away and she looked at him as if…as if what he said and did really mattered to her.

That was something, outside of his inter-actions with Jesse, that he hadn't had in a long time, either: to feel as if he mattered. Up until this moment, he hadn't realized how much he liked that feeling. Now he understood it was probably behind his initial decision to stay on in Star City. It was good to be valued, especially at Christmastime.

"Are you going to cut his hair or not?" a man in the group around them called out.

Addie shook her head as if to bring herself back to the task at hand. She held up the shears again and plopped a can of shortening down on the table. "You ready, Mr. Goodlife?"

"For anything, Mrs. Goodlife," he said with a smile. Then he added, "But I do have one last request."

She paused with the shears above his head. "I guess every man in your position deserves that. Ask away."

"If I do end up looking like the poodle next door, promise me you'll get me a really nice hat for Christmas."

She paused for only a moment. Then she smiled, a bit sadly, and said, "I promise. I'll do whatever I can to make sure you get what you really want for Christmas."

Chapter Ten

Since she was already in costume and ever eager to grab her share of the spotlight, Bivvy stepped up and took on the role of Goodwin's salesclerk in the webisodes they filmed not long after Addie finished Nate's haircut.

"He looks pretty cute all done up like a 1959-type guy, don't you think, Mom?" she asked as Nate and Jesse mugged their way through the last of the two-minute spots that the foursome had improvised all over the store. Though they had only made ten of them, it had taken nearly two hours, and Addie was so tired she was looking forward to the tedium of puttering around her kitchen set.

"Well, he's a pretty cute fella," Bivvy said, plunking her elbow down on the glass countertop across the aisle from the electronic-toy display. "Which one are we talking about?"

Addie laughed lightly. She was going to say "Nate, of course," but when she turned and saw the two guys standing there, with Nate pretending to need Jesse to explain the basics of computer gaming and Jesse eating it up, she shook her head. "Both of them, I guess."

"Have you given any thought about what you're going to give them for Christmas?"

"Yes, and I'm not telling you." Addie made a slashing motion, the sign of zipping her lips. "You'll blab."

"I will not." Bivvy, who had her glasses, that pencil and for all Addie knew a partridge in a pear tree in her hair now, folded her arms. "But just for saying that I've half a mind to not tell you what they're getting you."

Addie laughed. Bivvy pouted a bit, then gave up and broke into a chuckle, too.

"Okay, so I am no good at keeping a secret." She walked around from the back of the counter to stand beside Addie, whom she nailed with a steely-eyed glare. "Like mother, like daughter."

"Me?" Addie scoffed. "I didn't tell you anything."

"You don't have to tell me a thing,

sweetie. It's written all over you." She pointed her finger, now with a fire engine–red nail, at Addie and made tiny circles. "You're in love with Nate Browder."

As if he had heard his name spoken, the man turned, smiled right at her and then started walking in her direction.

Addie's heart leaped. Love? She'd known him less than a month. He was California-bound, and she was a Star City citizen through and through. He was a standout in everything he did, and she was...

She brushed her trembling fingers over the snowflake clasped to her headband. Suddenly she couldn't stand to think another second about who she was and what might have been. So, in order to change the subject, and preferably to something that would make her mother hush, she blurted out, "I got Jesse one of the snowglobes with the silver snowflakes inside of it that they sell in the gift department here in the store. You won't tell, will you?"

"Addie, honey, I know you think I'd do anything to draw attention to myself, but I would never give away your most precious secrets."

Addie exhaled, but it didn't really ease the pressure in her chest. "Thank you, Mom."

"Even if I think you are foolish not to own up to those secrets when they are right there for anyone who has ever been in love or who just has eyes in their head to see."

Nate strode up, with Jesse tagging along behind. "Eyes to see what?"

"How cute you two are, darlin'." Bivvy crinkled her nose at Nate and then Jesse.

"Yeah." Addie smiled, weakly, ducked her head and then made her getaway. "I have to go now. I have to demonstrate how to make manger animals out of common household items."

After the changes, the time seemed to fly the following Monday. Bivvy was a big hit, and as a result of her appearances on the Goodwin's site, her votes in the Web contest had skyrocketed. That got her house on the local news all the way over in Knoxville.

The Goodwins, though tight-lipped about business, seemed happy with the results. Doc, getting a lot of interest in the vintage goods used in the promotion, was even looking into going through all the junk he had warehoused in the now-vacant part of the Goodwin's building. Addie didn't know if that was a good sign or a bad one. Maybe he had finally resigned himself to the fact that the place was going to close, and his son, whose investment time-wise in Jesse could have been measured in minutes rather than days or hours this week, didn't care what happened to his family or his family's business. That broke Addie's heart for the Goodwins and for Jesse.

That feeling grew each day when, at shortly after five o'clock, Nate pretended to come home from the office and she and Jesse greeted him with open arms. That part was not pretend, they were actually glad to see him and know the three of them would be spending the next few hours as a family. It was the kind of thing that Addie hadn't known since before her father died. But at least she *had* known that kind of love and shelter. For Jesse and Nate it was a completely new, and obviously welcome, experience.

With that in mind—and not at all because of what her mother had said about her being in love with Nate—Addie decided to make their last regular day together special. Before the chaos of the Open House all day on Saturday and their parting on Christmas Eve morning, she thought these two special guys in her life deserved an evening as a family.

So she had asked Doc to allow them to stay behind in the store for an extra hour or so after closing, with the cameras off, so that they could have a quiet "family" evening.

"Don't tell Maimie," he said, dropping his keys into her cupped palm. "You take as long as you want, but stay in the front area so you won't show up on the alarm system's surveillance cameras."

It didn't take any great persuasion to get Nate to linger. He was babysitting Jesse anyway while the Goodwins—Doc and Maimie, Darin and his new wife—went out to dinner to discuss the subject of the child of Darin's first wife, whom he had legally adopted but did not want.

"I know we're not supposed to trim the tree until tomorrow," Addie said as she kicked off her heels and undid the wide black patent-leather belt she had worn all day.

"I can't wait to do the tree!" Jesse went up to the spot they had picked out to put the large fir they were going to bring into the store to decorate throughout the day. "I wish we had one now."

"Me, too, Jesse," Addie said, truly sad that they didn't have one.

"Ask and you shall receive!" Nate came

into the living-room set with a two-foot-long rectangular box tucked under his arm. "One Christmas tree, fresh from the forest of junk in the warehouse."

"My provider!" She clasped her hands together, went up on tiptoe and, raising one foot, planted a kiss on his cheek.

"Nate's the best!" Jesse slid the box out from under his arm and plunked it and himself down in the middle of the oval carpet.

"I went over and found it on my—" Nate turned his head unexpectedly "—lunch break."

Addie found herself staring right into those earnest brown eyes, and she knew. Her mother was right. She did love this man. She looked away quickly before he knew it, too.

"Hey, this isn't a Christmas tree." Jesse dragged the contents out of the box, littering the rug with a silver stick with predrilled holes and a pile of tinsel-covered branches wrapped in brown paper. He tugged one of them free, and the gleaming fringe sprang out in a shiny whale-tail pattern. "It's pink!"

"It might not be the right era." Nate shrugged. "I just went for the oldest-looking box I could find."

"It's all right. We'll make do."

"Yeah, but it's not perfect," Nate said quietly. "This is the first Christmas I've actually tried to celebrate in a long time. I kinda wanted it to be perfect."

"A perfect Christmas?" Addie rolled her eyes and laughed. "Why would you want anything that boring? The only really perfect Christmases are the ones that turn out nothing like you planned. That catch you by surprise. That remind us that we're messy, imperfect humans, and for a time, because He loved us so much, God became one of us. Isn't that the coolest thing ever?"

"The absolute coolest," he murmured, brushing a wayward strand of pink tinsel from her hair.

They set up the tree, but since it couldn't have lights they had to make do with directing a large flashlight, the kind that made a sort of spotlight, at it. And since the ornaments were already in boxes waiting to be brought out in a big production tomorrow, they had to make do with what they could find.

"Wait, I know what we can use." Addie went to the kitchen and gathered up red plastic cookie cutters and some stylized copper cooking utensils. "I won't need these anymore, since we're not doing demos tomorrow."

They laughed and joked and hung them all around. Nate sacrificed the skinny green tie he'd been wearing to the "office" and Addie contributed her patent-leather belt for makeshift garlands. Still, when they stood back Jesse looked glum. "It needs something for the top."

"I have just the thing!" Addie undid the snowflake from her headband. "It's not very big, but it's very special. Just like you, Jesse."

She clipped the pin to the top of the small tree that was barely as tall as she was, then they all stood back and admired their work. Addie couldn't help thinking of all the lights and decorations at her mother's house right now. And how she wouldn't trade a tenth of them for this corny, cluttered mess of a pink Christmas tree shared with two people who had come to mean so much to her. "You know, I think this is the nicest Christmas tree I've ever helped decorate."

"Me, too," Nate murmured, coming to her side.

For just that one moment the world was calm and peaceful and...wonderful. Nothing existed beyond the three of them and their improvised celebration. No jobs. No job interviews. No Goodwin's. No tomorrows. Just now and each other.

"This actually *is* kind of perfect, isn't it?" Nate asked in a whisper.

"Yes." Addie nodded, her hair rasping against his shirt. "But the thing about this kind of perfection, the *imperfect* kind of perfection, is—"

"Now what?" Jesse's tennis shoe squeaked on the floor as he spun around and started looking around for something more to do.

"It never lasts," Addie concluded with a laugh. She moved away from Nate reluctantly and plunked her hand on Jesse's head to get him to settle down and listen to her. "You know, in my family we didn't just put up the tree." Addie took a deep breath, then exhaled to remind herself that the moment had passed and she had it in her to move on. "We also made a big deal of setting up our big outdoor plastic lighted crèche."

Nate held his hands out to his side. "I didn't think to look for one of those."

"Good thing that in the Goodlife family, the man is not the only provider around." She gave Jesse a wink. "The box with all the things we made this week is in the cabinet under the fake sink."

In a matter of minutes, Nate was sitting cozily on the couch while Jesse and Addie knelt on the rug to better set up the homemade Nativity scene on the coffee table before them.

"It's not as showy as the one my mom has, but I like it." For the past week, Addie had been methodically assembling the pom-pom sheep, thread-spool cows and pinecone angels dipped in glitter with net wings adorned in sequins. There were felt shepherds with yarn hair and beards and that star with the spray-painted macaroni, too.

One by one they set each piece where Jesse thought they looked best in the Popsicle manger.

"Before my dad died we used to make a big deal out of the holy family's spot in the Nativity. We'd read the story out of Luke, then my mom would set Mary in place, my dad Joseph and I'd get to put in baby Jesus." Addie looked at the last three delicate figures. Made of chenille and sparkling metallic pipe cleaners, they had faces cut from vintage-style Christmas cards. "I still look at our crèche, even in the middle of all the craziness my mom has set up on our front lawn, and I remember that salvation didn't come to us in a big showy display, but simply and humbly."

She carefully placed Joseph and Mary, but when it came time for baby Jesus, she looked at Nate and then offered the small bundle to the little redheaded boy at her elbow. "I think you should do the honors."

Jesse took the last figure in the palm of his hand and held it.

Nate gave the boy a nudge. "Put the baby in the manger, pal."

He looked up at Nate and made a sour face. "I get the shepherds because there are sheep and angels because it's Christmas, but why did they put a baby in a box of hay?"

Addie and Nate exchanged glances. Then she put her hand on the boy's back. "Don't you know the story, Jesse?"

He looked up, so somber. "I know it's Jesus's birthday, but I don't know why they put him in hay."

"Because there was no room for them in the inn," Nate explained patiently.

Addie thought about trying to recite the story from the Gospel according to Luke, but Jesse seemed more interested in talking about the baby and His situation.

"No room? But Jesus was just a baby." He looked at the bundle in his hand. His voice grew thin and strained. "Didn't they care what happened to Him? Didn't anybody care enough to take Him in?"

Addie wanted to cry. She knew the boy was empathizing with the Christ child in a way that she never had. She reached out and pulled Jesse into her lap, stroking his hair to give him whatever comfort she could, even if it was just for this one special night. "That's the great gift of Christmas, sweetheart. Even though people rejected and mistreated Jesus when He was here, even though they reject Him to this day, He came here for us."

Nate moved across the couch to where Addie was sitting on the floor with Jesse. He put one hand on her shoulder and the other under Jesse's chin. "Because of Jesus, everyone is welcomed into God's family."

"I'd like to have a family," he said softly, his eyes down as he finally placed the baby figurine in the manger to complete the scene.

Addie shut her eyes, and a tear rolled down her cheek. All she knew to say was, "I'm praying that you have that, too, Jesse."

After that nobody felt much like celebrat-

ing. Addie thought about suggesting they
open gifts, but she knew it would only feel
awkward, and she wondered if maybe, in
time, that was what they would remember
more than the small circle of special time
they had shared this night.

And so they moved their mixed-up tree to
the kitchen, then gathered up their belong-
ings. After locking up, Addie dangled the
keys out for Nate to take, since he'd be
seeing the Goodwins tonight. "Give these to
Doc, and don't let Maimie see."

"I'll do it," Jesse said.

"Okay." She gave them to the boy, then
planted a kiss on his cheek. "Get plenty of
sleep tonight. We have a big day ahead of
us tomorrow."

Chapter Eleven

The Open House was a huge success. The oldies radio station did a great job setting the mood with Christmas songs from the 1950s. Tons of people showed up, many in costume. Women wore everything from poodle skirts to aprons and pearls to movie-star glam, and men dressed like Elvis, beatniks and dreamboats.

At times there were so many people in costume in the store that Addie couldn't help imagining that was how it must have looked during that first Christmas season years ago. She kept busy serving cookies and punch and didn't even shy away when people asked to have a picture taken with her.

The day went by quickly, and just after six, as the sky grew dark and the lights all over town began to come up, they put the finishing touches on the huge live tree. They had decorated it according to a photograph of one of the Christmas trees that the Eisenhowers had had in the White House. Everyone oohed and ahhed over it.

"I liked ours better," Nate whispered as he dropped into the couch next to her and pointed to the little pink tree tucked away in a corner of the kitchen set.

"Ten, nine, eight…" The crowd began the countdown to the big light up.

"I liked ours better, too." *Ours.* Addie liked saying it, even if she knew it could never be.

"Seven, six, five…"

Doc stood at the ready with an extension cord in one hand and the plug from the lights of the tree in the other.

"Four, three, two…"

Jesse came up to Addie and Nate, exhausted, and crawled into Addie's lap. She hugged the boy tightly, thinking that even though it would all be over soon, for just this one moment she had everything she'd ever wanted for Christmas.

"Merry Christmas, Goodlife family," Nate said to the two of them.

"Merry Christmas," she whispered back, trying not to tear up.

"One! Merry Christmas everybody!" the crowd cried in unison as Doc pushed the plug into the extension cord socket and…the whole store went dark.

Not just the store, but parts of the downtown, as well.

A moment of confusion followed.

Addie held Jesse close to her so he wouldn't get hurt in the shuffle of customers.

Doc went to the front of the room and flipped on all the switches they had dimmed to better highlight the tree.

Nothing.

"I'm afraid that might be my fault." Bivvy rushed forward, noticeable even in the dark with her jingle-bell earrings jingling and Christmas-trimmed party dress flashing. "Since I've had my house online and gotten TV attention, it seems more people have decorated this year, and a nice man from the electric company told me it's been causing brownouts in small segments of town at a time."

The crowd grumbled.

Goodwin's security guards moved swiftly to the front doors to keep people from rushing to them. Everyone was asked to come to the front area of the store, to stay calm and wait while a call was made to the

Star City Electric Company to see how soon they could restore power.

People began to shuffle and complain.

Jesse slipped from Addie's lap. She made a grab for him but came up empty-handed.

From somewhere in the crowded store a child bellowed, "I want to see the tree. It's not like Christmas without a tree!"

"In our family, we make a big deal about the crèche." A small boy's voice rose above the low rumble of the restless group. Then a bright halo of light illuminated the coffee table and the Nativity scene that Addie and Jesse had made over the past week.

The whole room fell silent.

Nate put his arm around Addie. She put her hand out to the little redheaded boy. Jesse came to her, and after she pulled him close she began to sing, softly, "Away in a manger, no crib for his bed…"

And in a moment the whole crowd had joined in singing softly but clearly in the stillness of the powerless night about the baby who had come into the world so humbly that He had no place to lay His head.

Once they had finished singing that, someone else started another song. And after that another.

Jesse moved from the table to the place where Doc and Maimie had planted themselves beside the front doors and slid his hands in theirs.

"What did I tell you?" Addie said to Nate as they sat side by side on the couch surrounded by the sweetness of the moment that no one, no matter how hard they worked behind the scenes or how much they stood out from the crowd, could have orchestrated. "It's the *im*perfections, the unexpected, that make Christmas special. It's being caught off guard by—"

"Love," Nate finished for her.

"I was going to say joy, but love is good," she murmured. The flashlight gave off just enough brightness so that she could see his face.

"Love is very good."

With the darkness to give them privacy, Nate put his hand behind Addie's neck and kissed her. Not the fleeting kind of kiss she had given him under the mistletoe the first time they met, but a real kiss. The kind of kiss that could change the whole way a person saw her world.

Or the way the whole world saw her.

Just then the lights came up. Not just the

ones on the giant tree but all the lights that Doc had flipped on when the power first went off. It was as if spotlights and searchlights had been thrown on Addie and Nate. Kissing.

A cheer went up.

Addie stood, looked around at all the happy faces staring at her.

"That's my girl!" Bivvy said in a show of motherly approval.

The group laughed.

Addie's head spun. Nobody here was ever going to take her seriously. She would always be Bivvy's daughter or Maimie's lackey or the girl caught kissing the guy who flew off to California. Her heart raced.

Nate reached over to take her hand, but she jerked it free. She had to get out of there. She had to breathe. She pushed past the coffee table, the customers, the Goodwins. She pushed her way out the front doors and ran as fast as her aching feet could take her.

Chapter Twelve

Nate stood up.

"What just happened?" Doc asked.

Nate held his hands out to show that he had no idea why Addie had run off. He went back over what had been said. He'd told her he loved her. And then she kissed him, which meant she felt the same way, right? And then she'd bolted out the door.

He stood there shaking his head.

"Go after her!" Maimie pushed the door open for him.

"Hurry." Bivvy gave his shoulder a light shove.

"Really?" He took one stumbling step, then halted. "I think maybe she just wants to be alo—"

"Go!" the whole crowd chimed in unison.

"All right! I'm going." He reached into his pocket to make sure he had the Christmas present he had planned on giving her tomorrow, then headed to the front of the store.

"I'm going, too!" Jesse rushed ahead of him to the open door.

"Hey, pal." He lifted the boy up to speak to him eye to eye. "Not that I don't appreciate the backup, but this is kind of a one-man job."

"Yeah. But I'm not a man, I'm a kid." He poked his thumb into his chest. "It's a one-man-and-a-one-kid job."

Nate could not look into the eyes of a kid he had just tried to teach about God's love of us all and say he wasn't welcome. "Okay, put your wheels down, we have to move fast."

They took off down the road in the direction she had taken the first day when she had left the store. When they reached the corner, Nate wasn't sure which way she might have gone.

"Her house is that way." Jesse pointed across the street toward the residential area a couple of blocks down.

"You think she went home?"

"Duh! She went to look at the Nativity scene on the lawn." Jesse had already started rolling in the right direction.

Nate caught up to him in a few steps. He didn't see her anywhere, but Jesse pointed out that she probably knew a shortcut. Though he'd been by the McCoy house and certainly seen it on the Internet. "You know, pal, now in the dark, I'm not sure I can pick out Addie's place. Seems like a lot of houses are really lit up now."

"Not like *that* one." Jesse went sailing toward the house on his wheeled shoes, then stumbled to a stop, turned back and, eyes wide, made his opinion of the sight clear. "Who-o-oa!"

Nate's gaze fell on the lone figure of Addie sitting by the Nativity, the glow of all the lights illuminating her beautiful face.

"I couldn't have put it better myself, pal." He gave the kid's shoulder a firm pat to tell him to stay put, then went to her. "Addie, I—"

"I'm so humiliated." She hung her head. "Everyone is probably talking about this right now, laughing at Bivvy McCoy's daughter, who acted like a perfect romantic goof."

"Naw." He knelt beside her on the lawn and gave her shoulder a nudge with his. "Nobody thinks you're perfect."

She whipped her head up and glared at

him, her lips set thin, her eyes brimming with tears.

"But that's why I love you." He reached out and took her hand. "Perfection is overrated. It's the unexpected that makes everything special."

"You…did you just say you *love* me?" She blinked, and this time the tears spilled over onto her cheeks.

"Yeah. I thought I'd made that clear before we kissed back at Goodwin's." The look of complete shock on her face told him that he hadn't. "Then I guess it will really surprise you to find out I got you this for Christmas."

He reached into his pocket and pulled out a small red velvet box, which he flipped open.

"Oh, Nate!" Her hands trembled as she reached out and took the box. She tilted it slightly, and the lights around them glinted off the simple diamond solitaire inside. Her shoulders shook. She kept her face down. A small whimpering-type sound came from her, but nothing more.

"Addie?" He swallowed to try to clear the lump rising in his throat. "What are you thinking?"

She raised her head at last, tears streaming now, and smiled even as she blubbered, "I only got you a hat!"

She threw her arms around his neck.

"Is that a yes?"

"Yes!"

Nate busted out laughing and wrapped her in his embrace.

At that Jesse came running up to them. When she saw the boy, she let out a small gasp. "What about Jesse? I hate the idea of going off to California and leaving him here."

Nate put one arm around the kid's shoulders and gave his bride-to-be a smile. "We'd hate that, too, seeing as I'm not going to California."

"You're not?" She sniffled, the ring box still in her hand and the ring still not on her finger.

"Nope." Nate remedied that by slipping it out of the satin-lined holder and taking her hand in his. "I'll tell you the details later, but it's enough to know right now that I'm going to be working in this town for a very long time to come. So if you still want to go to California…"

"I don't!" She slid her finger through the ring he had held out, then threw her arms around him and kissed his cheek.

"Aw, you can do better than that," he said.

"You kissed me better than that the first day we met. Of course, nobody was watching then."

"Hey, *I'm* not watching now." Jesse covered his eyes and turned his back. "Not if you're going to do *that* stuff!"

Nate chuckled, took Addie in his arms and kissed her properly.

Chapter Thirteen

The next day passed quickly for Addie, what with all the rush of congratulations and the rearranging of everybody's Christmas plans and the fact that she felt that her heart now actually had wings.

Nate had caught her up on the decisions that had been made at the dinner between the Goodwins. Maimie and Doc intended to become the boy's legal guardians. Though they knew they couldn't take on raising him, they would assume responsibility for his needs and set up a trust fund for him. Meanwhile Nate would continue to care for him, and after they were married and ready for the responsibility, the Goodwins hoped they would take the boy to raise themselves. Though Nate would have to have help, as he intended to go back to school to become a child and family therapist, in Star City, of course.

As for the future Mrs. Nate Browder?

"I can't believe the Goodwins are putting me in management training," Addie said as she and Nate and Jesse walked out of the early evening candlelight service at Addie's church together.

"Hey, somebody has to learn the business to teach Jesse here when it's his turn to take over." Nate ruffled the kid's red hair.

Addie smiled. "Who knows what Goodwin's will look like then? If there will even still be a Goodwin's?"

"If there is, fifty years from now I hope they do a promotion where they show typical life for us now." Nate guided them toward the sidewalk. "Where the dad raises the kid and the mom runs the business."

"And the baby Jesus is still the most important part of Christmas," Jesse added.

Addie gave the boy a hug, then looked up toward the brightly lit houses of her mother's neighborhood. "Mom's caroling party for people who want to walk together to the midnight service doesn't start until ten. Tomorrow morning we're all going to the Goodwins' for Christmas presents and brunch. But I'm not sure what we should do right now."

"Let's go home and just be a family," Jesse said.

Nate and Addie looked at each other, not sure what to say except, "Jesse, the three of us don't have a home."

"Sure we do!" He dug deep into his pocket and pulled free the keys that Doc had given Addie and that Addie had given Jesse to give back to Doc.

Nate laughed. "Do we dare?"

"With Doc's keys we can turn off the alarms and no one will ever know," she said, beaming up at the man she loved. "And if they do know, who cares?"

And that was how they came to spend Christmas Eve at Goodwin's Department Store, with their love and the joy of family and the wonder of the unexpected blessings of Christmas on display for anyone to see.

* * * * *

Dear Reader,

Blessing of the season to you and those you love! I come from a long line of folks who love Christmas and celebrate it to the hilt, so our home is always done up in decor that includes old family treasures from as far back as the forties. The idea for having a couple fall in love in a 1950s setting, however, came from the Johnson County Museum's 1950s All-Electric House, which had a living display of a family Christmas circa that time frame.

It became all the more fun when I imagined using an old department store inspired by one in the real town of Georgetown, Kentucky. Now whenever I go through there I think— Hey, there's Goodwin's! There's the church where they have the Nativity. That's the way to Addie's house! Yes, that's how real the characters have become. Of course, that is thanks in part to the fact that I could give them a spiritual dimension that recognizes and rejoices in the greatest gift of all, the birth of our Lord and Savior, Jesus.

Happy Holidays!

Annie Jones

QUESTIONS FOR DISCUSSION

1. If you could experience Christmas in another time period, when would it be?

2. Addie and Nate were on display, but they also had a chance to put their faith on display. How do you think their faith showed up in their behavior?

3. Do you have a special Christmas tradition that is unique to your family? Please describe it.

4. Are you more of the kind of snowflake who likes to stand out or the kind who likes to blend in? What type do you think Addie is? Why?

5. Do you have neighbors who decorate as enthusiastically as Bivvy does for the holidays? What do you think of them? How much do you decorate for Christmas?

6. Do you have an ornament or decora-

tion that enriched Christmas for you?
What is it, and why do you find it so
special?

THE CHRISTMAS LETTER

Brenda Minton

This book is dedicated to the readers.
Thank you for the encouragement, the letters and
the prayers. Many blessings and merry Christmas.

For unto you is born this day in the city of
David a savior, which is Christ the Lord.
—*Luke* 2:11

Chapter One

"No, no, no. If she doesn't see that he's using her, she doesn't deserve him." Isabelle Grant wadded up a piece of paper and threw it at the television.

"Mom, it's a movie." Lizzie stood at the door, long, dark hair pulled back in a ponytail. When she wore it like that, she still looked like a little girl and Isabelle didn't feel thirty-three.

But her daughter was twelve and getting older every day. Lately it seemed as if they had changed roles. Lizzie was forgetting that Isabelle was the mom and she was the daughter. Isabelle clicked off the television and stretched. She had to be at the Hash-it-Out Diner, Gibson, Missouri's one and only restaurant, in thirty minutes, for the evening shift. And Lizzie, as on so many evenings, would be home alone. At least they had a great neighbor in the duplex next door. Mrs. Jackson kept an eye on things.

"I know it's a movie, but the characters should still make wise choices."

"Yes, wise choices. I remember that lecture."

"Cheeky kid." Isabelle hugged the child, who had sat down next to her on the sofa. "I love you."

"You know, Mom, I think you might be addicted to the Hallmark Channel."

"That was Lifetime."

"Whatever. They're all the same."

"Are not."

"Sappy movies and docudramas."

"Okay, so what would you prefer me to watch?" Isabelle drew one leg up and turned to look at the child who was blossoming into a beautiful young woman. She wanted to stop the clock, to keep it from happening.

For a long minute, Isabelle felt alone, really alone. She ached deep inside, reminded that someday Lizzie would spread her wings and fly away to her own life, her own dreams, her own happy endings.

Isabelle prayed there really would be happy endings for her daughter.

"Mom, I don't care what you watch. I just wish your life was about more than those movies. You should go out on a date."

"I don't need to date." Because she had loved the best man in the world, and he'd been taken from her.

"You need to do more than work and raise me."

Isabelle looked hard at her daughter. "When did you grow up?"

"Last year. I'm preteen now, remember?"

"Yeah, I remember. And you'll be thirteen in March."

"And I really, really want to go to the dance camp in Tulsa. I asked Jolynn, and she said I could help her clean house this winter. She'll pay me. I can save money, and you won't have to work another job."

Big sigh. Isabelle *so* did not have the money for dance camp. But maybe, if she could do more bookkeeping at home in her spare time, or work an extra day at Ed's Garage on the outskirts of Gibson, where she was a mechanic. But if the extra money went to camp, how would she take care of Christmas, just a month away?

"Mom, don't look so worried. I know we might not be able to afford it."

"But I *want* to afford it, Liz. I really want to give you everything."

"You're always telling me that we don't get everything we want in life."

Isabelle closed her eyes, remembering that lecture, the one she gave when she didn't have the money to give her daughter everything she wanted to give her. Moms didn't get everything they wanted, either. Sometimes dreams were expensive.

"I love you, Lizzie." Isabelle hugged her daughter close. "And now I have to hurry or I'll be late. Jolynn will have my hide."

"No, she won't."

The doorbell rang. The two looked at each other. Isabelle peeked and couldn't see who was on the front stoop. "Are you expecting someone?"

"Nope."

Isabelle glanced out the window. A truck was parked in the drive. A new truck. "Oh, goodie, I think we've won a new truck. That has to be it."

She opened the door, leaving the chain in place. Gibson, Missouri, wasn't dangerous, but that didn't mean she had to be careless. A man stood in front of the door. A man in a military uniform. His presence took

Isabelle back, but in her memories it wasn't a soldier on her step—it was a police officer. Thirteen years, and she still remembered that night. She could still feel the rip of pain that tore through her heart as the officer told her that her husband had been killed in a car accident.

She could still remember holding her belly, where the unborn Lizzie was safe, not knowing that their world was falling apart. She remembered telling the trooper she didn't have family to call. The officer had called Jolynn, because he'd known her from church.

The soldier on her front step cleared his throat and smiled. Man, he was gorgeous. His dark hair was shaved short, and his skin was tan from too much time in the sun. When a smile broke across his face, dimples split his cheeks and white teeth flashed.

"Surprise!"

She blinked, because, yes, she was surprised, but she didn't have a clue what he meant by that. Maybe she'd won a soldier, not a truck? Behind her, Lizzie gasped, and then her footsteps retreated down the hall to the bedroom.

"Surprise?" Isabelle didn't want to sound like an idiot, but she was clueless. Had she met him before? Had she entered a sweepstakes, and the prize was a soldier for Christmas?

She unhooked the chain and opened the door the rest of the way.

"I brought you something." He smiled again and held out a bag. "Sand from one of the holiest sites in the world."

He handed her the bag with a ribbon tied around the top. She blinked a few times and tried to think of something to say. Asking him who he was would have been a start.

"Isabelle, are you okay?"

No, of course she wasn't okay. She had to go to work. Tonight after work she and Lizzie were going to cut down a tree for Christmas. A stranger had just handed her a bag of sand, and he knew her name.

How could this be right?

She looked at the name on his uniform. Daniels. The name sounded familiar but she didn't know anyone in the military.

"I'm sorry, do I know you?" When she asked the question, he frowned.

"Well, I guess you don't, not really. But after a year of writing letters, I guess I thought…"

"Whoa, wait a second. Writing letters?" Isabelle wanted to sit down. She glanced at her watch. She now had fifteen minutes until she had to be at work. She remembered a letter, last year, a Christmas letter. She hadn't written it, though.

"Letters, Isabelle, and packages. I just processed out of the military, and thought I'd stop and say hello."

"Letters?"

His hazel-green eyes were staring at her like she was a crazy woman. "The letters you wrote to me…or maybe didn't write."

"Lizzie, front and center." Isabelle thought about letting him in, but she wasn't going to let him into her home. She didn't know if he was really a soldier. He might be the crazy one, not her.

Lizzie slunk down the hall. Her face was pale, her brown eyes huge. And she had that look on her face, the one that made her look more like her father and less like Isabelle. The guilty-but-sheepish look.

"Mom, I can explain."

"Please do."

"I should come back." Chad Daniels spoke, backing off the stoop.

"No!" Isabelle and Lizzie said at the same time. The soldier looked like retreat might be his best option. Though he didn't look like a guy who retreated. He looked like a hero to Isabelle. And she couldn't go there.

Isabelle took a deep breath to compose herself. It didn't work. "Wait. We'll figure this out."

"I'm the one who was writing to you." Lizzie turned from pale to pink. "Our class sent packages to Iraq, and when we got the letters back, I got a letter from you. And you sounded like a really great person. You sounded…"

The Christmas letter. Realization dawned slowly, and Isabelle wanted to groan as the pieces of the puzzle came together.

She waited for her daughter to finish, but Lizzie didn't. Instead her eyes overflowed with tears, and she bit down on her bottom lip. "I'm really sorry."

"How did I sound? I mean, other than sounding like a great person." Chad stood at ease on their sidewalk, tall and with shoulders so broad they stretched the desert-sand camouflage of his uniform tight across his chest. His gaze, serious but gentle, was fixed on Lizzie.

Isabelle leaned against the door frame and waited for her daughter to answer. Lizzie glanced from the soldier to Isabelle and then back to the ground, her teeth biting into her bottom lip. Finally she looked up. Her brown eyes overflowed with tears, and she sniffled.

"Like you needed a friend." Lizzie looked from him to Isabelle and that's when she knew what her daughter had done and why.

"Oh, Liz, you shouldn't have." Isabelle covered her eyes with her hands and wished the ground would swallow her. "I have to go to work."

"I guess I have to leave."

"There aren't a lot of places to go," Lizzie offered, a tentative smile back on her face. "I mean, you could go to Springfield, but you weren't looking for a city, you were looking for a real town, a community. There's a bed-and-breakfast here, just down the road. It opened up last year."

"Lizzie, stop." Isabelle stared at the soldier—a man, not a boy.

"I think I'll drive around Gibson and decide what to do." He smiled again, and he didn't look lost or confused. Those emotions were Isabelle's, obviously. "Lizzie, you're a great kid. I really enjoyed our letters. I'm a little embarrassed now, but that's okay. You did a sweet thing, wanting two people to be a little less lonely."

He saluted and walked away, long strides, strong and in control. Isabelle's insides were shaking, and she didn't know what to do next.

But she had to go to work. As the truck drove down the street, she turned to face her daughter. "I can't believe you did that. I'm a grown woman, Lizzie. I don't need to have my twelve-year-old daughter arranging my love life."

The truck turned the corner, and she wondered if she had seen the last of Chad Daniels. Not that it mattered.

But if it didn't matter, then why in the world did it make her feel sad? Only one reason made sense. She felt sad for him. It was nearly Christmas, and he'd come to town thinking he'd find a friend. Instead he found that he'd been tricked. By her daughter.

"You have to apologize." Isabelle grabbed her purse and gave her daughter a look that Lizzie knew well. "You can't play with a man's emotions that way. It isn't fair."

Life isn't fair. One of the many lectures she'd given in the past. Sometimes life even hurts. Officer Chad Daniels probably already knew that.

* * *

Chad drove to the parking lot of a deserted old gas station. The concrete was cracked, and weeds had grown up and then died in the cold of winter. Cold. He liked that feeling. He liked the damp, brisk air that smelled like wood smoke from fireplaces and drying grasses, maybe a little fertilizer from a nearby farm.

But now what? He'd been writing to a kid for nearly a year, believing she was a woman. An adult woman. His face warmed, and there wasn't anyone to witness his embarrassment. He could only imagine what the guys in his unit would say. They would have teased the old guy who had gotten duped by a kid. His face burned a little hotter. He rolled the window down all the way.

Those letters had taken him into the life of a woman he'd never met. Isabelle—dark hair, dark eyes and unspoken dreams that she had never shared. Her husband had died before the birth of their first child, Lizzie.

The real author of the letters, that child.

He smiled a little, because the kid had spunk. He should have seen it in the letters, the sometimes childish scrawl in her handwriting. He should have known it was a girl, not a woman.

But it was Isabelle's story, her life, that had brought him here. The stories of a town that took care of its own had drawn him to Gibson. A town that helped a widow, raised money when someone was sick or provided when a family lost their home to fire—those were the things he wanted.

He had been in a foreign country fighting for towns like Gibson to stay safe, to remain in their peaceful cocoons where Christmas was still about a Nativity in the park and "Silent Night" was sung during a community gathering. He had been fighting to give that freedom to towns in a foreign country, to people who had dreams of their own.

Lizzie might have written the letters, but the town of Gibson was real. He had fallen in love with a community he'd never known before her letters. He wanted to meet Jolynn and eat pie at the Hash-it-Out Diner. He wanted to watch the lights come on during the annual Christmas Lighting Festival, held the first Sunday in the month of December.

Somewhere deep inside he admitted that he wanted to get to know Isabelle Grant, because her smile had been the first thing he thought of when he touched American soil two months earlier.

A car pulled up behind him. Lights flashed blue, and the door opened. A young cop, tall and cautious, got out of the car. Chad reached into his back pocket for his license.

He was ready for the officer, but the guy didn't take the paperwork. "I don't need those. I saw you sitting here and thought you might need help. There's a garage down the street."

Ed's Garage where Isabelle worked three days a week, changing oil and fixing small mechanical problems.

Chad read the guy's name tag and smiled, because he felt like he knew the people in this town, thanks to Isa... No, thanks to Lizzie's letters.

"Thank you, Officer Blackhorse. I'm fine—just needed a minute to think. Is there a hotel in this town?"

A hotel? Why would he do that? He could drive on to Florida, where his parents had moved last year. He could visit a buddy in Colorado. He was forty, retired, and he could go anywhere. Why would he stay here, in a town where he didn't know a soul? Okay, he knew two souls, but didn't really know them.

"You okay?" Officer Blackhorse leaned closer, peering into the truck, surveying the contents. He looked relaxed, but Chad noticed that his right hand remained on his weapon.

"I'm fine." He pulled off his hat and tossed it onto the seat next to him. He might as well tell Jay, the guy that had recently gotten married to the waitress, Lacey Gould. Chad actually had pictures of the officer's wedding. "I got played by a kid. I've been getting letters from a woman, but they were letters from her daughter. I think it might have been an attempt at matchmaking."

"Lizzie Grant?" Jay Blackhorse grinned.

"That's the one. I wanted to meet the woman behind the letters."

"Cute kid, but a little feisty. Isabelle has her hands full. That girl is her life, though."

"So I should leave town?" Chad looked down the main street of Gibson. A truck with a lift bucket had stopped by a light pole, and a city worker was stretching Christmas lights across the street. It had been three years since he'd had a real Christmas.

"I wouldn't leave if I wanted to stay." Officer Blackhorse rubbed the back of his neck and followed Chad's glance to the street ahead of them, the stores, the cars lined up in parking spaces. "If you're looking for a temporary residence, there's a bed-and-breakfast, the Pine Tree Inn. If you want permanent, I have a house for rent in the country. And there are places to buy."

"Why don't you direct me to that bed-and-breakfast, and then maybe we can get together and talk about the house in the country."

He was retired. He wanted to have some land, a few horses, some cattle. He'd been dreaming this dream for three years.

"Directions. I can do that." Jay pulled a pen and a small tablet out of his pocket. "Here's the address and directions to the Pine Tree. And my phone number if you need anything."

"Thank you, Officer Blackhorse. I'll be seeing you around."

"I'm sure you will. Oh, and if you need a meal, the Hash-it-Out Diner and the convenience store down on the corner of Main and Highway 15 are about the only places in town."

Chad nodded and started his truck. Jay Blackhorse backed away from the truck, still grinning. Chad waved as he pulled out of the parking lot.

He was staying in Gibson. He couldn't explain why. Maybe because he didn't have another plan. Maybe because of dark brown eyes and a winter sky that looked heavy with snow. And he hadn't seen snow in a long time.

Chapter Two

Isabelle tied the apron around her waist and took another sip of the cola she'd poured when she arrived for work. Jolynn, owner of the Hash-it-Out, slipped behind her and into the waitress station, mumbling about the waitress who hadn't refilled the ketchup bottles before she took off on some hot date.

"She's young." Isabelle defended the waitress, feeling lighthearted in spite of her daughter's huge mistake coming to light. A year of letters, starting last Christmas. Only a few, Lizzie had assured her. Because they had written to soldiers for a school project the previous year, and Chad had written back to her, sounding a little sad, a little lonely.

"What's up with you today?" Jolynn lifted the big ketchup container and started to pour ketchup through a plastic funnel into the squeeze bottles that they kept on the tables.

"Nothing." How did she admit that a man had shown up on her doorstep?

"Oh, honey, I've seen that scrunch between your brows before. That isn't a sign of nothing. That's a sign of…" Jolynn grinned. "That's a sign that your daughter has been up to something. I love that girl. What did she do this time?"

Isabelle covered her face with her hands and shook her head, trying not to laugh…and not to cry. "Am I really so pathetic, Jolynn?"

"Well, honey, not in my book. But I imagine if you tell me the story, it'll make sense from the perspective of a twelve-year-old."

"She's been writing to a soldier and signing my name."

"Now, isn't that sweet. That isn't so bad, is it?"

"He showed up today."

Jolynn's mouth opened, as if she had planned to say "Oh," but nothing came out. Her eyes widened, and then her chest heaved a little. Laughter bubbled up from the older woman, and tears trickled down her cheeks. She set the ketchup bottle down and wiped her eyes with the corner of her apron.

"Oh, Isabelle, that's about the funniest thing yet. I do love that girl."

"You would take her side. Jolynn, I can't let this go. I mean, I know she did it because she loves me and she thought it would be romantic." And in a way, it was. If she hadn't been embarrassed—no, mortified—she might have been touched. "She needs to be grounded or something."

"I'm sure she's sorry."

"Not as sorry as she should be."

The cowbell over the door clanged. Isabelle slipped an order pad in the pocket of her apron and grabbed a glass of water.

"Take care of the customer. I'll figure this out," Jolynn said as she went back to pouring ketchup.

"Come up with something good. I'm at the end of my rope with that girl."

"I'll come up with something good. And I'll keep her busy working, and that'll keep her out of trouble."

Jolynn winked as Isabelle turned and walked out of the waitress station.

It really did take a village to raise a child. Isabelle smiled at the thought, because the town of Gibson had loved them and cared for them since Lizzie's birth. The child had more aunts, uncles and grandparents than any other child Isabelle knew.

She headed for the table by the window. The customer looked up, and Isabelle stopped. She didn't groan, but she wanted to. Chad smiled and dipped his head in greeting. That smile was dangerous. He shouldn't be allowed to do that in public, not in the presence of unsuspecting women.

"Isabelle." He put the menu down. "What do you recommend?"

Leaving town was an option, but she didn't say it, just smiled at the thought. "Depends on what you like. I love Jolynn's cashew chicken. Other people like chicken-fried steak."

"I'll have the cashew chicken. No cashews. I'm allergic."

"Got it. One chicken and rice."

"I'm really sorry about today. I guess I shouldn't have just shown up like that, knocking on your door without warning."

"I'm not sure how you could have made the situation any better. And I'm the one who has to apologize, for what Lizzie did."

"Don't. She was great, trying to help two people, you and me. Sweet girl."

"Yes, sweet and sneaky."

"You said she…" He stopped and shook his head. "Nope, that was her, telling me she's a beautiful dancer."

It was funny, Isabelle couldn't deny that, and she even laughed. Her daughter didn't mind tooting her own horn. "Yes, she's a dancer, and really quite talented. She wants to…"

"Wants to what?"

"Nothing. I'll put this order in." She turned away from him, because he wasn't a friend or someone she knew. He was a stranger who had shown up on her doorstep. A stranger who knew things about her life. How much did he know?

Heat crawled up her cheeks again.

"Hey, before you leave, I wanted to tell you, she didn't mean to hurt either of us."

Isabelle turned. Lizzie had hurt him. She hadn't thought about it like that, about him being hurt by the letters. What had he expected to find when he came to Gibson?

"No, she didn't mean to hurt anyone."

"Good, I'm glad you agree. Oh, I was told that the owner of this café, Jolynn, has a B and B with a vacant room."

Isabelle started to laugh. Of course the inn had vacancies—it was in Gibson. Who came here? Sometimes families in town had company and no extra beds. That was about it.

"Yes, she has vacancies. I'll send her out."

Jolynn was waiting inside the waitress station. As Isabelle rounded the corner and slipped past her, the owner of the Hash-it-Out was leaning against the counter, fanning herself with an order pad. "Wow."

"Stop." Isabelle poured a cup of coffee for their customer.

"Honey, you don't need to punish that girl of yours. You need to give her a medal for bringing that man to town. If you aren't interested, I can tell you someone will be kissing him under the mistletoe before the month is over."

"He wants to talk to you." Isabelle lifted the order. "I'm taking this to the kitchen."

As she walked away, she was imagining him under the mistletoe, and it wasn't a stranger in his arms. She shook off the vision. She really needed to stop watching those movies.

Jolynn was a motherly woman with her hair dyed light blond, and coral lipstick that framed her smile, making it bigger and brighter. Chad could see why everyone in the community loved her, including Lizzie. Because it was Lizzie who had written the glowing things about her mother's employer.

Jolynn helped them through rough times, brought them to her home for Christmas and never let them eat Thanksgiving dinner alone. Instead she had a big dinner at the restaurant for people who didn't have a family to gather with.

One more thing he had loved about Gibson, as he had compared it to his childhood and the many times it had been just his mom, his siblings and himself, eating dinner and waiting for his dad to call.

When Chad had picked the military as a career, he had made a decision not to marry. He had kept his heart intact by never dating a woman more than a few times, never letting himself really get to know her.

The letters from Lizzie, letters about Isabelle and her daughter, had been the longest relationship of his life.

He hadn't really thought about it as a relationship before, but now he realized that he knew more about her than he knew about anyone else, except maybe the guys in his unit. As an officer, he had known a lot about his men, their families, the problems they faced. No one had really known him. Until he had shared his dreams with a girl who wasn't Isabelle Grant.

He had shared that he hadn't really known his dad.

Isabelle had shared that Lizzie had never known her father. She had encouraged him to talk to his dad. He was forty, and a twelve-year-old posing as her mother had done that for him, because she would have loved the chance to know her dad, to talk to him just once.

He leaned back in his chair, still holding his coffee cup, not really thinking about where he was, or who was watching.

"Hey, soldier, how's that coffee?" Jolynn sat down across from him like she'd known him his entire life.

"It's great coffee, thank you."

"Well, that's good to know. I like a good cup of coffee, myself. Now, how can I help you?"

"I'm looking for a place to stay, maybe a month or so. I'm not sure yet…"

"Not sure where you're going to land?"

"Exactly. But I do like the idea of spend- ing Christmas in Gibson."

"It's a good place to spend the holidays. Or

even to stay for a lifetime." She winked and poured more coffee from the pot she had carried out with her. "Don't get in a big hurry. Just pray and let the Good Lord guide you."

"I'm not in a hurry." He leaned back in his chair. "I guess, for the first time in years, I've got nowhere to go."

"Sometimes a person needs that." She smiled, her eyes so kind he felt like he could tell her anything. For a guy who never told anyone anything, that was a strange moment.

"Yeah, it isn't so bad."

"I have a nice suite that I think you'd be comfortable in. Before you leave, I'll give my husband a call and have him meet you over there so he can let you in."

"Does it have a kitchen?"

"Oh, no, but I provide breakfast here at the restaurant every morning, and you can help yourself to whatever is in the fridge. I don't mind if you cook something up, either. As long as you clean it up when you're done."

Who did that? Chad now knew the answer: Jolynn. She opened her home and obviously her heart up to strangers. And hopefully no one would ever take advantage of that fact.

The kitchen door opened, and Isabelle

walked through the swinging double doors. She paused, holding a plate that steamed. Her dark hair was held back in a clip, and the black apron was hitched low on her hips.

Isabelle, a foster child who had married a boy she met in a group home and then was widowed before her daughter's birth. That was one of the things he knew about her. But it wasn't something she'd told him. Now everything that he knew felt like whispered secrets that she hadn't shared. The pink in her cheeks was understandable.

He felt that thud of letdown, because he had really thought they would be friends, that they were already well on their way to friendship. And now she was a stranger.

"Here's your supper." She held the plate and carried a pitcher of water. "Did you get things worked out with Jolynn?"

Her employer stood, and as Isabelle put the plate down in front of him, Jolynn slid an arm around her shoulders and gave her a light squeeze. Chad wondered how long it took a person to become a part of this community. He had a feeling it took about five minutes.

"We worked it out," Jolynn answered. "Oh, and I forgot to invite Chad to the Christmas program at the firehouse this Sunday night."

"The first Sunday of the month," Chad finished for her. He had purposely shown up in town this week because he didn't want to miss that program.

"Yes, of course you know that." Jolynn filled his cup again. "And church is at eleven on Sunday morning."

She hurried away, leaving him alone with Isabelle, who shifted from foot to foot, her gaze not connecting with his.

"I'll have you over for dinner some night," she offered. "We should do something to make this up to you."

"You don't have to. It was all an innocent mistake. One Christmas letter and a chain of events. No big deal. It did bring me here, and this is a little bit of what I've been looking for." Maybe his entire life.

"I know, but I do feel bad."

He didn't want her to feel bad. He wanted her to be a friend. "Okay, if it'll make you feel better. I heard you make a great roast."

"Lizzie." She sighed, but then she nodded. "Okay, roast it is."

Chad watched her walk away and then dug into the chicken and rice, as she'd called his cashew chicken without the cashews. And he thought about Sunday and how

wrong it was for him to pursue this relationship. Worse, he kept thinking that he didn't
want to wait until Sunday to see her again.

Chapter Three

Isabelle was off work on Fridays. And today, because of morning snow, Lizzie was out of school. It didn't take much snow for Gibson to call off classes. She and Lizzie had spent the morning doing laundry and cleaning house. Then they'd made chocolate-chip cookies.

Now it was late afternoon and they were going to watch movies, with the house still smelling like cookies and the spicy scent of the candle Lizzie had lit. Isabelle curled up on the couch and waited for Lizzie to change into sweatpants.

Isabelle wanted something to take her mind off the man that had invaded her life, eating at the restaurant every day for the last four days—since the day he'd arrived in Gibson.

"I start my job at Jolynn's on Monday." Lizzie plopped onto the couch next to Isabelle. "Chad's living there, she said."

"Yes, he moved in right after he left here."

"Don't you think he's cute for an old guy?"

Isabelle flipped through the channels, trying to find something romantic and sweet but safe for a twelve-year-old. "I don't think he's old."

"He's forty, and he's never been married."

"Lizzie, you shouldn't know these things about his life. We haven't really discussed this, but it was wrong of you to write those letters. Really wrong." Isabelle's stomach turned a little at the thought. "It's wrong, and you could have gotten him in trouble."

Lizzie bit down on her bottom lip, and her eyes narrowed with worry. She was a sensitive little soul. "I just wanted you to meet him. He was so nice when I wrote to him, and I told him about you and our life here."

"And then *I* started writing to him." Isabelle wanted to be amused, but the sick feeling in the pit of her stomach won out over amusement. "It was a lie, and you used that poor man."

"He was lonely, too. You're both lonely."

"I'm not lonely. I have you." Isabelle picked a movie, a teen romance that she'd seen more than once. "I have an entire town of people who love me."

And she disliked every activity between now and the new year because she would spend them all alone, or as a single mom. There'd been a few times in the past friends had tried to fix her up on blind dates, and a few offers from single men at church. She'd turned them all down because she was too exhausted with work and being a mom to date. But Lizzie didn't need to know that.

"You don't have someone. Everyone should have someone. I'm not going to be here forever, you know."

Twelve. Isabelle had to remind herself that her daughter was twelve. "No, you won't be. But even when you're gone, I'll be fine."

"What if I go to camp for a month?" Lizzie's mouth was a straight line of seriousness.

"I'll be fine. I'll work. I'll have my friends."

Lizzie nodded in the direction of the television and the movie just coming on. "You'll have movies and a box of tissues."

Isabelle grabbed the remote off the coffee table, bumping her tea glass and nearly tipping it. She turned off the movie that started with a pretty college student tripping all over herself when a cute guy said hello.

"Lizzie, no more. We're not going to keep talking about this. I'm the adult. You're twelve. I really do know a little about life, and about what makes me happy. You make me happy. Your attempts at matchmaking—not such a happy moment for me. Especially when your matchmaking lures some poor guy to a town where he knows no one. As a matter of fact, I want one last letter from you to him. A letter of apology."

Lizzie's bottom lip was between her teeth, and she nodded. "I can do that. And you're right, I shouldn't have interfered. I just wanted…"

A dad. Isabelle knew what her daughter wanted. And if either of them said it, they would both cry. Lizzie wanted to know the man that she could only identify through old photographs. Dale, a young man with dark hair and a small scar on his cheek. He'd been Isabelle's knight, a tall, skinny kid who had worked hard and always managed to smile.

He'd had a habit of finding the good in every situation. A lot like his daughter, Lizzie.

"When are we going to get our tree?" Lizzie crawled up next to Isabelle and snuggled close. "It isn't rainy or snowy today."

"Maybe tomorrow morning. You know I don't like to drive on these roads."

"Okay." Lizzie flipped the television back on and changed from the movie to a cartoon. But even the cartoon squirrel had a boyfriend.

The low rumble of an engine grabbed Isabelle's attention. She leaned back on the sofa and peeked outside. Chad Daniels, in her driveway. Isabelle shot her daughter a look—in time to catch Lizzie sucking in a smile that had nearly escaped.

"I hold you personally responsible for this, my little chick." Isabelle kissed her daughter's forehead. "Not only have you complicated my life, but you've ruined sappy movies for me."

"That's because the real thing is better." Lizzie did smile then. "You've been hiding in those movies for years, Mom. It's time you experienced real life, and maybe some real romance."

"I have a life." She had already had marriage. Now she had a daughter, two jobs and hands that were dry from dishes and too much cleaning. She also had a gray hair. She'd found it last week when she'd given herself a trim.

But Chad was knocking on the door, and

she didn't have time to continue the discussion with her obviously unrepentant daughter. Or the thoughts about the life she was convincing herself she possessed.

This was crazy. Chad stood looking at the green door with the Christmas wreath hung over the window, and he knew he'd lost it. He was forty, his palms were sweating and he had a chain saw in the back of his truck.

Not because he had gone crazy, but because he had experienced a sudden burst of Christmas cheer.

"Hi." Isabelle stood in the doorway.

It took him a minute to recover, because she was beautiful in sweats and a T-shirt. And she was standing in front of him, her feet bare and dark eyes serious. He had been in town for a few days now, and he knew more about her than any woman he'd ever known. She liked hot chocolate with peppermint sticks, and she cried when the choir sang "Amazing Grace." He had learned that from Jolynn's husband, Larry, who thought of Isabelle as a daughter, the child he'd never had.

"Hey?" Lizzie peeked over her mom's shoulder, her smile huge. "What are you doing here?"

"I'm, uh…" Floundering. He sighed, because this wasn't him, this person who had lost control. He had retired as a lieutenant colonel in the army. He had served during war. He knew how to command troops and bring them home safely.

He didn't know how to deal with this woman or the child standing behind her.

"Here for cookies?" Lizzie offered.

"No. Actually, I came by because I knew you were planning to get a Christmas tree, and I happen to have an extra one in my truck."

"You have an extra tree?" Isabelle said in a way that made it incredulous, not a question.

"I went out to look at the Berman farm today, and Larry and Jolynn asked if I would cut them down a tree while I was there. I went ahead and cut down two."

Her dark brows shifted up, and she laughed. "What if we already have one?"

"I'd give it to Jolynn's neighbor. Mrs. Sparks hasn't decided yet if she wants a tree." He winked, because he enjoyed watching her get flustered.

"She always waits until the week before Christmas." Isabelle motioned him inside, rubbing her arms after she pushed the door closed. "Are you staying in Gibson?"

Did she care? He wondered if he wanted her to care.

"I'm thinking about it. I went out to look at the Berman farm. It's a shame they have to sell."

"They're moving to Springfield. They have kids up there, and it's getting hard for the two of them to care for that much land."

"It would be a lot of work to keep up with a place that size." One hundred acres and a two-story farmhouse with four bedrooms. He had made an offer. "About the tree?"

"We can have it. Right, Mom?" Lizzie was hopping a little, peering over Isabelle's shoulder. "We were going to have to get one anyway."

Chad turned his attention back to Isabelle, and he could tell she was struggling with the decision. Her teeth worried her bottom lip, and she was staring past him, where he knew there was nothing to look at. Finally she nodded.

"Okay, we'll take the tree. Will it fit in here, or do we need to trim it?"

"It'll fit." He pulled his gloves out of his pocket. "I'll bring it in."

"We can have hot cocoa and cookies while we decorate. Mom makes the best homemade cookies." Lizzie's smile split across her face, infectious and sweet.

"Does she?" He smiled at Isabelle, but she didn't smile back. "I'm really just here to drop off the tree."

"You have to stay and help us decorate. What fun is cutting down the tree if you don't get to at least put the lights on it?" Lizzie glanced from him to her mother.

"Lizzie, I'm sure Chad has somewhere else…"

He shook his head. "No, not really."

Decorating the tree hadn't been part of his plan, but now that he was in her living room, close to her, he wasn't ready to leave.

"Okay." She gave Lizzie a look that he was sure she hadn't planned for him to notice. "I'll go find the decorations, if you want to bring in the tree."

"I'll put cookies on a platter and find the star. I think I put it in the hall closet last year." Lizzie slid out of the room on her stockinged feet. What kid wouldn't want to slide on hardwood floors?

"Good idea." Isabelle's gaze lingered on the door even after Lizzie was gone.

"She's a great kid. I hope you've forgiven her."

Isabelle turned. "Of course I have. She owes you an apology, though. I explained to her how wrong it was for her to deceive you that way, and the troubles it could have caused. She's young."

"I know she is. But it wasn't such a bad thing. I'm here, and Gibson is the town I thought it would be. It isn't a complete loss."

He rubbed a hand over his face and groaned, because that hadn't come out the way he'd planned. The guys in his unit had been right about one thing: he was inept when it came to women.

Isabelle touched his arm, the gesture surprising him. There was a lot about her that surprised him. Like the fact that she'd remained single. "At least you got the town you were looking for."

Her hand moved back to her side, and she walked away, leaving him in the living room, alone. He glanced around, taking it in, this real picture of who she was and the life she'd lived.

One thing he knew from this room was that she loved her daughter. There were school photographs of Lizzie, one for every year of school. Eight pictures, starting with a five-year-old girl, brown hair in pigtails.

On the bookcase was a photo of a young couple holding hands. She wore a wedding dress and had stars in her eyes.

He turned away from the photograph, because it was too personal. And it connected dots, the things Lizzie had shared in letters signed with Isabelle's name.

He walked out the door, thankful for the cold air of early December. He pulled on his gloves and lowered the tailgate of his truck to pull out the tree. Six months ago, this town and this house had come to life, painted by the words written by a twelve-year-old girl. Now he was here, and he didn't know why he had stayed.

But then again, maybe he did. Because the real Isabelle, the woman standing at the window watching him, was more captivating than the letters written by her daughter had made her out to be.

And Gibson felt more like home than any place he'd ever been. No matter how he'd gotten here, it felt like the place where he could live the rest of his life.

Isabelle opened the door as Chad pulled the tree toward the house. She stepped back, laughing when the monstrous cedar got stuck in the doorway. Lizzie cheered him on, telling him to turn it a little to the right. He grunted and tried her suggestion.

"Do you think it might be too big?" Isabelle asked as he gave it a heave and pulled it into the living room. She closed the door behind her and pointed to the corner where she'd put down the tree skirt and the stand.

"I measured it. It's six feet tall."

"But it will be taller once we get it in the stand."

"And put the star on top." Lizzie stood, hovering at the edge of the action.

"I think it'll be fine." He smiled over his shoulder, and Isabelle knew that he didn't believe it. He knew it wasn't going to fit.

"While you get it set up, I'll untangle the lights."

"Untangle?" He pulled the tree to an upright position, lifted and set it in the stand that Lizzie was holding.

Isabelle held up the strands of lights, but kept a cautious eye on her daughter. Lizzie was screwing the bolts into the tree trunk while he kept it in position. What would Lizzie do if he left? If he decided not to buy that farm or stay in Gibson?

"We should have put the lights back on the

holder they came off." Isabelle looped the lights back through an opening in the cord. "We never do, though."

"That is a mess. If you wait, I can…"

"I can do it." Isabelle kept working. "And the tree is too tall."

"It'll be fine. Look at how full it is." He motioned with his hand, like she'd won the prize on a game show.

"It's perfect." Lizzie looked up from her position on the floor, screwing in the last bolt of the tree stand. She stood, backing up to look at the tree. "There's a little bare spot, but we can turn it and it'll be great."

She turned the tree and stepped back by Isabelle.

"Yes, it's perfect. Here are the lights. I'll start the cocoa."

Because she couldn't do this with Chad Daniels. She couldn't stand next to him, stringing lights on a tree, not with the photograph of Dale on the bookcase reminding her of the two Christmases they had shared—and all of the ones without him, when it had been just her and Lizzie.

Chad smiled at her like he understood. Chad in a red flannel shirt and jeans, his work boots laced up, covered in red-clay mud.

Mud. She looked at her hardwood floors, the dried mud showing the path he'd taken. "Your boots."

He looked down and groaned. "I'm sorry. Get me a broom, and I'll clean it up."

"No, don't worry about it. I'll sweep it up. You two put the lights on the tree."

He grinned, flashing those white teeth. And his eyes sparkled with humor. "You want out of untangling this mess."

"Exactly." And she escaped, because that's what it was really all about.

From the kitchen she could hear their laughter, her daughter's and Chad's. He was giving her directions, his voice low and gentle. Lizzie chattered about the decorations they used. The ones they'd bought and the ones they'd made.

Isabelle stirred water into cocoa, added sugar and a dash of cinnamon and then mixed it into the milk on the stove. She poured in a little vanilla and kept stirring. The aroma of the cocoa lifted as it began to steam. And Isabelle tried not to think about her daughter decorating the tree with Chad, and not her.

It had always been just the two of them, Isabelle and Lizzie. This had been what they did together for years. Decorating the tree had been their moment, their time and their memories.

This year Christmas included a stranger, a man brought into their lives through letters her daughter had written. Isabelle turned off the stove and walked back into the living room. She stood at the door and watched as Chad took the star from Lizzie and placed it on the top of the tree. That had always been Isabelle's job. Things changed. Life changed. She knew that and sometimes even told herself to prepare for it. This hadn't been one of the scenarios she had played out in her mind—this man, Christmas. Her star.

He was standing precariously on the stool, and Isabelle had to smile, because he was cute and Lizzie was hovering like she might catch him if the stool tipped.

"Don't fall," Isabelle warned.

He wobbled a little and grabbed, steadying himself with one hand on the wall. "Thanks. I'll be careful."

He put the star in place, plugged it into the lights and then nodded at Lizzie. She plugged in the cord, and the tree lit up, just lights and a star, no decorations yet. But it was pretty in the dark, shadowy room with the sky outside hovering between gray and white as dusk fell, no sun to set because clouds had kept it hidden all day.

"Help us hang the decorations, Mom." Lizzie held out the round bulb that Isabelle hung every year. The one she'd bought the year she turned eighteen, when she and Dale had married.

They had married the week they left the group home they'd spent their seventeenth year living in. Before that they'd both been bounced around from foster home to foster home. Through those tumultuous teen years they'd kept in touch, keeping one another's spirits lifted through letters and phone calls.

She'd been the daughter of a drug addict who overdosed when she was ten. He'd been the son of abusive parents who could never really get their lives together enough to be parents.

And now, here Isabelle was, a single mom. But she had survived, and Lizzie was having the childhood that Isabelle and Dale had planned for their daughter.

Chad took the decoration that Lizzie held and handed it to Isabelle. "Come on. I cut it down, you have to decorate. That's your job."

She smiled a little, and it wasn't easy,

because her eyes were flooding with unshed tears, and his eyes were soft with compassion because he knew her stories. She didn't know how much he knew, but she was positive Lizzie's letters had shared too much.

But not the things Lizzie didn't know. There were things she would never know. Isabelle met his warm gaze and saw something in the dark depths of his eyes. He had stories, too. She wondered if he would ever tell them to her. Or why a man followed letters to Missouri.

"Thank you." Isabelle didn't look at the decoration in her hand. She knew that it had a picture of the Nativity on one side and a verse on the other. And in her heart she knew that Chad Daniels wasn't going to share his stories.

"Put it here, Mom. In the middle." Lizzie pointed to what she thought was the perfect place, and Isabelle nodded and hooked it in place. The pungent odor of cedar filled the house, mixing with the leftover scent of fresh-baked cookies, making it smell like Christmas.

"We need Christmas music." Isabelle's throat was tight with emotion, and she turned away from the curious gaze of the stranger who had invaded their lives.

"And we need hot cocoa so we can finish."

Lizzie hung a red ornament and then a gold one. "I'll fill our cups, and you finish this."

Isabelle flipped on the television and turned to the satellite station with Christmas carols. "Okay, but be careful."

"I'll be careful, Mom. I won't burn myself."

Chad laughed a little. "It's a never-ending job, isn't it?"

"What?" Isabelle handed him a small box of ornaments.

"Being a parent."

"Yes, it's never-ending. But I wouldn't trade it for anything. You've never…" She didn't know anything about him.

"No, never been married, never had a child. I was a military brat, and I made the military my life. I guess it was a comfortable place for me. It's what I know."

"That's honorable." And she now had pieces of his life, making it a little more even, since he had most of hers in letters she hadn't written.

He shrugged and hung an ornament up high. She stood back, away from him. "I loved my career. Now it's time to find something else to…"

She wondered if he had planned on saying *love*.

He smiled as he stepped back from the tree. "Something else to do. I've always wanted to have a farm."

"Really?" She had wanted that, too, but she felt old sharing that dream with him.

"Yep. My grandfather was a farmer in Nebraska. We didn't get to see him often enough, but I always loved the time we spent there."

She'd never really known her grandparents, either. But for different reasons. Her family was dysfunctional as far back as she could remember. She'd learned stability from the foster family that had kept her, the last foster home she'd been in. They kept her until she turned seventeen, and then they'd left the state, and she had hoped they would take her.

They had written, but she hadn't seen them again.

"Lizzie says you're a mechanic." He said it like he couldn't believe it.

"Trade school. We had to pick something, so we both…" She glanced at the picture of herself and Dale. "We picked the automobile field. I picked mechanics. He picked body repair. We were going to start a business."

"I'm sorry." His hand rested on her arm,

and she couldn't move away from the tenderness of his touch. It was warm, that hand on her arm, and strong.

She hadn't expected that touch to mean something. She let out a deep sigh and brushed away tears.

"It's okay. It was a long time ago." And she had Lizzie.

Speaking of Lizzie, she was singing along to the radio, a song about Christmas cookies. It was George Strait, and they both loved George.

"We should get busy, before she thinks we've been..." Chad laughed. "Sorry, that wasn't what I meant. But I do think she means for us to decorate the tree."

"She does." Isabelle pulled out a small box of ornaments she and Lizzie had made with baked dough and acrylic paints.

"I like this one." He held up an ornament shaped like the manger. "We decorated our tree with paper snowflakes last year. Let me tell you, I'm not good with paper and scissors."

"What's it like over there?" She wondered if he had shared the stories in the letters he'd written, the letters she hadn't read or even seen.

"It was good, watching the progress. Sometimes it was a heavy load, keeping the people in my unit together, keeping their spirits up."

"Have you always gone to church?"

"Didn't you read…" He laughed. "No, you didn't read the letters. Lizzie, could you tell your mom when I became a Christian?"

"He was thirty-five and in Afghanistan with a crazy Christian kid in his unit who wouldn't stop praying. And they were always safe with that kid praying." Lizzie walked into the room carrying a tray with three steaming mugs of cocoa.

"There you go." Chad smiled and shook his head. "That kid is now twenty-five and a youth minister in Texas. I guess he was never a kid."

"Cocoa and cookies." Lizzie put the tray down on the table. "Let's take a break."

As if she was the adult chaperoning two kids. Isabelle looked up, meeting the soft, warm gaze of the man that her daughter had brought into her life. This wasn't a movie, or a book. It wasn't a fairy tale.

It wasn't a first date.

And what she felt, fluttering inside her heart, getting trapped in her lungs, was all about this moment in time, about his smile, the way his hand had felt on her arm.

It was about her own loneliness, something she'd been trying to deny for a few years. It had sneaked up on her, waiting until she was done with diapers, sleepless nights and those first few years of school to rear its ugly head. But she kept busy, with work, with Lizzie, and she convinced herself she didn't have time for relationships.

"About church on Sunday." Chad sat down with a mug of cocoa and a cookie. Lizzie choked on her cocoa, and Isabelle looked up, afraid of what this meant, and afraid to let her daughter believe that this could be everything she wanted it to be.

Or maybe afraid to let herself believe.

"Yes, church."

"Since I've crashed your tree-decorating party, what if I just meet the two of you at the town lighting ceremony Sunday night?"

"Yes, that would be good. Everyone will be there." Isabelle hated that she sounded like a chicken. But meeting at the lighting ceremony was safe. It was public. It wasn't about two people brought together by one little matchmaker.

Chapter Four

Sunday evening Chad walked down the sidewalk from Jolynn's to the metal building that served as the fire station for the Gibson all-volunteer fire department. He wasn't the only one walking. There were groups of people walking together, and families with children. Every parking space was filled, including the parking lot of the Hash-it-Out.

The fire station was next to the small city park, and he could see the lights that had been strung up. Tonight was the night those lights would be turned on for the first time. And houses that had been decorated would be lit up as well. He had helped Larry decorate the Pine Tree Inn that morning.

He had asked why they did it this way, the entire town lit up for Christmas on the same night. Larry said it was about community. It was about Christmas being about Christ's birth and not watering it down by lighting up two months early, so that by Christmas, no one noticed anymore. And the central part of the lighting ceremony was the Nativity in the park.

This ceremony was a community worship service, not just a ceremony about lights or displays.

The weather had cooperated by making it feel like Christmas. The air was brisk, a little damp, and wood smoke billowed from the chimney pipe that stuck out of the fire-station roof. Chad stopped to watch the crowds, his gaze landing on a familiar figure, a tall brunette with a nearly teenaged replica at her side. They were both wearing plaid jackets and caps. The door to the building opened, letting out a swath of light and the sound of laughter and conversation. They moved through the door with a group of people that he recognized from church.

He walked through the door alone, not a part of any group or church. But he'd been to church that morning, to the little community church attended by half the population of Gibson. He had sat behind Isabelle and

Lizzie, watching as mother and daughter, heads bent, discussed something in soft whispers. He had listened as the pastor spoke about God's gift of love in the form of His son, Jesus.

Chad had sat in that church, feeling as if he'd been attending there all his life, thanks to Lizzie's detailed descriptions in her letters.

And now he was at the lighting ceremony. He stepped into the metal building that wasn't quite warm, even with the fire in the woodstove. People stood in groups, dressed for the weather in heavy coats and gloves. He greeted a few of the people he'd met around town, and then he searched the crowd.

"She's over here, soldier." Jolynn hooked her arm through his. "I'm so glad you stayed in town. This is a good place to put down roots."

"I haven't quite decided if I'm staying."

Jolynn patted his arm, and he noticed that she had painted her nails red and green for the occasion. "Where else would you go?"

"My parents live in Florida."

"That's a good place, too. But Gibson,

well, I moved here about thirty years ago, and I couldn't imagine living anywhere else."

Neither could he, but he wasn't ready to tell that to the owner of the Hash-it-Out. He smiled, and she nodded toward a group standing in the corner of the building, near fire equipment and extra hoses for the truck that had been backed out of the building for the night.

"Our church choir is over here. Come on—we need a good tenor, and if I heard right at church this morning, you're just the guy."

"Well, I don't think I'd say I'm a 'good tenor,' but if you're not picky, I can fill the part."

"You'll do just fine."

As he walked up to the group, Isabelle smiled a shy smile, and the impact of the gesture hit him square in the gut. Or maybe near his heart. A smile had never made him feel like that, and he definitely didn't consider himself a romantic kind of guy.

So why had he come to Gibson, looking for Isabelle Grant, a woman who watched romantic movies on TV and cried when she read books with happy endings?

"Here's the guy we've been looking for." Larry, Jolynn's husband, held out a song sheet. "They assigned us to sing 'Beautiful Star of Bethlehem.' Do you know that one?"

"I think so." Chad read over the lyrics, and somehow, as the group moved, he got pushed to stand next to Isabelle.

"My daughter started a conspiracy," she whispered, smiling a little, laughter twinkling in brown eyes. He knew she was talking about the way the two of them were being pushed together. "They mean well."

"I know they do. Do you think I mind standing next to you?" In the closeness, his shoulder brushed hers.

"Do you mind the gossip of a small town?" She kept her gaze straight ahead.

"Not at all."

Another church group moved to the center of the room, and the crowd grew quiet as they started singing "Silent Night." Chad stood at Isabelle's side. Children, not interested in singing, were sitting on the floor or playing in groups. A baby cried.

He remembered a year ago, singing carols with the men in his unit around the tiny tree they'd decorated. And he remembered a letter from a young girl in Gibson, telling him about her Christmas, her mother and this celebration.

Six weeks later he'd received that first letter signed with Isabelle's signature.

The song ended, and another church group moved forward.

Standing next to him, the real Isabelle, not the letter, not the image he'd created, shivered as the door opened and another group of people entered. He shrugged out of his coat.

"Here, take this." He draped it over her shoulders.

"I'm fine. It was just the draft when the door opened. And you'll need it when we go outside."

"I have on a heavy sweater." He held the coat out so that she could slip her arms in. "There you go. And to be honest, I enjoy the cold air."

Her gaze softened. "What's it like, coming back?"

"It's an adjustment."

"You came here, instead of going home to spend Christmas with family." There were questions in that statement, and he realized she didn't know him. Of course she didn't.

"If I go home for Christmas, it would be to Florida, where my parents live now. They have an active social calendar. They usually don't put up a tree, and Christmas dinner is at a restaurant. I came here because of the letters. I wanted this for Christmas." He nodded at the crowd gathered inside the fire station.

"I understand. I couldn't imagine being anywhere else."

Jolynn motioned them forward. "Time to sing."

The group of about twenty moved to the center of the room. And Chad stood next to Isabelle, a part of the community, a part of the lives of these people. He'd always had the military community, and they were tight, but this was a place a guy could call home. Military life meant moving in and out of lives and communities.

At the front of the group candles were lit, and next to him, Isabelle sang in a soft soprano. The room was dark, and they stood in the center of the glow of candlelight, a song about a star of hope and promise echoing in the metal building. He could hear the people around them singing along.

Chad never wanted to leave Gibson, that feeling. His arm brushed Isabelle's. Their fingers touched, and he wondered if she would ever agree to more than a moment in public with him. Would she ever sit across from him in a restaurant, or tell him the stories that Lizzie had already shared?

At times he thought she might, but then she retreated into that shell, a place where he thought she probably kept memories of her husband and the shattered dreams the two had shared.

The song ended, and the candles went out. The group turned and left the center of the room as the overhead fluorescent lights came on. Their song had been the last, and the garage doors at the end of the building went up.

"What now?"

Isabelle smiled up at him. "The lights come on in the park and down Main Street, and then Santa rides in on the fire truck."

"Fire truck?"

"Well, of course, you can't expect him to drive a sleigh in Missouri." Her smile sparkled in her eyes, and someone pushed his arm on the other side.

"Hey, guess who's under the mistletoe." Jolynn pointed up.

Chad's gaze went up, to the twig of mistletoe hanging from the door frame. Isabelle groaned a little, her face upturned as she looked from the mistletoe to him.

"You have to kiss her." Lizzie was at his side, her grin mischievous and a little guilty.

"I don't think…" Isabelle bit down on her bottom lip.

"I don't think we can ignore mistletoe." Chad brushed her cheek with his hand, and her eyes closed.

Isabelle held her breath, waiting, unsure. She hadn't been kissed in so long, except by Lizzie. And tucking a child in at night wasn't the same as a breathless moment with a man whose eyes were warm and whose smile touched somewhere deep inside.

A hand on her cheek drew her back to the present, to the cool night air, the scent of cedar from the nearby Christmas tree, and Chad.

She opened her eyes as he lowered his head, and when his lips touched her cheek, she thought he sighed. The moment was sweet, and his hand was on her neck. When she thought the kiss would end with that innocent gesture, he moved from her cheek, barely grazing her lips. And then he pulled away, his gaze holding hers. Her breath caught in her chest, getting tangled with emotions she hadn't expected. It hurt, like thawing out after being in the cold too long.

But cold was good, because it brought numbness. This feeling hurt deep inside, where she hadn't hurt in so long.

A tear slid down her cheek, and she wiped it away with her gloved hand. The next one he caught with his finger, and then he kissed her again.

"I'm sorry," he whispered in her ear as he moved away. "But I'm not sorry for being here with you."

Christmas music on a radio, tinny-sounding but cheerful, broke the moment, and everyone moved away, forgetting them, forgetting the kiss. Everyone but Isabelle. She couldn't forget that moment when his lips had touched hers, or how his hand had been so gentle on her cheek.

The fire truck came up the street, blaring Christmas music, red lights flashing into the dark night, reflecting off the windows of nearby businesses. Santa was on the truck, tossing candy to the children and wishing them all the blessings of Christmas. And he had his dogs with him. Isabelle smiled, because everyone loved Santa and his dogs.

"He looks like Santa," Chad whispered. "What's up with the dogs?"

"We all call him Santa, and those are his

dogs. Dasher, Dancer, Comet, Cupid, Donner, Blitzen, Vixen and Rudolph."

"This is something our letter writer forgot to mention."

"She probably didn't think about it. He's been a fixture here for years. He's a retired minister, and he runs the local food bank. He might call himself Santa, but he knows the reason for Christmas is Jesus. He even made the Nativity for the park."

"I love it here."

"It's a great place to live. I'm always thankful that this is the dot we picked on the map, the place we decided to call home."

His fingers slid through hers, and he pulled her a little closer. Maybe because it was Christmas, or maybe because of the mistletoe, but Isabelle didn't pull away. Instead, she stood with him, watching as children grabbed up the candy that had been thrown from the truck.

After Santa's fire truck faded into the night, Isabelle turned toward the park, Chad's hand still holding hers tight. The crowd of people engulfed them, everyone moving together.

"Where are we going?" Chad leaned to whisper in her ear.

"Time for the lights to come on in the park."

People started to sing "Joy to the World." Isabelle blinked a few times, because this was the part where she always cried. This was like the happy ending of a movie, when it all worked out the way it was supposed to.

"Are you crying?"

She nodded but didn't look up, couldn't look at the man standing next to her. "I always cry at happy endings."

He gave her hand a light squeeze, and at that moment the lights came on. The entire town glowed with brilliant reds, greens and twinkling clear lights. The Nativity lit up with soft lights that were hidden behind the carved figures of Bethlehem.

And it was Christmas. Isabelle felt it in her heart, felt that moment when it all made sense, this season of rushing, buying, spending, sometimes worrying. This was what it was all about, this baby, this savior, and not the gifts or the rush, or the worry.

For this moment, everyone remembered. And she wished they could always remember and not lose sight of what was real, what really meant something.

"Come on, guys, time to go back inside for cookies and something warm to drink.

And door prizes. This year I'm going to win." Lizzie grabbed Isabelle's other hand, the one that Chad wasn't holding. And that left Isabelle between the two, between her daughter and the man her daughter's letters had brought into their lives.

"What do we do now?" Chad whispered in her ear as they walked through the big garage door, back into the fire station. The building was concrete floors and metal siding. Fluorescent lights hung from chains, and wood smoke scented the air.

"We go inside for door prizes."

"That isn't what I meant. What do we do now, after 'Operation Mistletoe'?"

Isabelle shrugged, hoping to pretend they didn't have to do anything. As if that kiss wouldn't be the talk of the diner tomorrow. She wanted to tell him it was Christmas and they were both lonely. That kiss hadn't been about them. It had been about the moment, the music, the lights and a sprig of green mistletoe.

"Why do we have to do anything?" She didn't look at him. They were threading their way through the crowds of people. "It's Christmas, and we're not the first ones to get caught under the mistletoe."

"I see."

She glanced up this time, because his voice was quiet.

"It's Christmas," she repeated and then searched for Lizzie, who had run off after they entered the building. "I hope she wins something. She deserves to win something."

"She's a great kid."

Isabelle laughed a little. "I'm glad you can see that, after what she did."

"She had good intentions."

"Yes, she meant well. But she shouldn't have."

"Isabelle, it's okay. She brought me here. I've found a place in the country that I can call home. The only thing I regret is that the friend I thought I'd find isn't really the friend I thought I'd been writing to for the last year. But that's okay. Maybe we can work on that part."

"I think we can be friends."

"Nothing more?" He had led her to the one quiet place in the building, and his eyes, dark and warm, studied her face with an intentness that made her look away.

Isabelle shivered and pulled his coat, a coat that had his scent, his warmth, closer around her. "Chad, I don't know about that.

I mean, my life is complicated. I have to concentrate on raising Lizzie, on working two jobs. Dating has been at the bottom of my list of priorities for a long time. I'm not even sure if I remember how."

"Maybe I can help you remember." He winked and still held on to her hand. "We could find that mistletoe again."

She smiled a little and moved her hand from his. "I think for now we should avoid the mistletoe."

Lizzie's shout that she'd won ended the conversation. Isabelle turned as her daughter ran toward them, holding leather work gloves and a can of coffee.

"I won!"

"You certainly did win." Isabelle hugged her daughter. "That's just what you've always wanted, right?"

Lizzie's eyes sparkled with laughter and youth. "You can have the gloves." She handed them to Chad and then held the coffee out to Isabelle. "And you get this.

"Merry Christmas." Lizzie stood on tiptoes, twelve-years-old and full of life. She gave Chad a loose hug. Isabelle liked that his face turned a little red and he wasn't quite sure what to do.

"We should go now." Isabelle shrugged out of his jacket and handed it back to him. "Thank you."

He took the coat. "You're welcome. And I'll see you tomorrow, right, Lizzie?"

"Yes, my first day of work. I'll be at the Pine Tree Inn after school."

Isabelle had forgotten, and now the reminder settled like a cold lump. Her daughter was determined to earn money for the dance camp that Isabelle couldn't afford. At twelve, she was determined and unwilling to give up on her dreams.

Isabelle prayed she wouldn't be let down.

Chapter Five

Chad parked his truck just as Lizzie Grant skipped up the sidewalk of Jolynn's inn. It was thanks to her that he was here. He finally had a hometown. He had signed the paperwork on the farm today, and in two months it would be his.

Lizzie, in jeans and with her plaid coat buttoned to the neck, stopped on the porch and waved, waiting for him. He got out of the truck, slipping his keys into his pocket as he walked. Lizzie, full of youthful exuberance, came down off the porch, her smile wide. She looked like her mother, tall and slim, with her dark hair long and pulled back in a ponytail. Her mom wore hers loose.

The main difference between mother and daughter was the expression in their eyes.

Lizzie's eyes were full of hope, full of laughter. Isabelle had lived a lot of life, and it hadn't always been easy.

"Hey, are you ready for your first day of work?"

Lizzie nodded and stepped next to him as he went up the stairs. "All ready."

"Your mom says you're saving for dance camp? It must be pretty expensive."

"It is, really expensive." She bit down on her lip and kept her gaze down. Like her mother. And he knew she wasn't telling the whole truth.

"Something tells me this is about more than camp." He opened the door and motioned her through, into the large Victorian with the polished oak woodwork and heavy antique furniture. The back sitting room, next to the dining room, was his favorite. The furniture in that room was leather and comfortable. Larry said that room was the one place in this house where he could really relax. The rest was Jolynn's doing. She liked frilly.

Lizzie obviously liked frilly, too. She went into the first room, the drawing room with furniture that was as comfortable as a wooden bench. The floors were covered with floral area rugs, and sheer white drapes covered the windows.

"What's up, Lizzie?"

She walked around the room, her back to him, touching the books on the shelves and then pausing at the porcelain figurines that lined the mantel. She finally sat on the edge of the floral sofa, her legs crossed at the ankles and her hands clasped in her lap.

"I want to buy my mom a Christmas present." She looked up, her brown eyes liquid and her smile a little tremulous. And he didn't know what to do. He'd dealt with tears before, with young soldiers who were homesick and wanted to go home, with new parents that hadn't seen their babies. But this, a twelve-year-old girl wanting to buy her mom a Christmas present, this was a new experience.

He cleared his throat and stood in front of her, trying hard to think of the right thing to say for this moment. She watched him, waiting, as if he was supposed to have the answers.

"What about camp? Your mom thinks you're saving money to go. And won't you be disappointed if you don't get to go?"

"I can always go to camp next year." She

glanced away, but not before he saw that look, the one that said she probably wouldn't get to go. "But my mom, she's given me everything. She's given up a lot that she wanted, so I could have what I want. She works two jobs so that I can take dance lessons. She's done all of that to give me my dreams, and I want to do this for her."

He sat down in the chair next to the sofa. "What is it she wants, Lizzie?"

"She's always talked about playing the guitar. She grew up in foster homes and never got to take lessons. It's the one thing she's always wanted. And working here, I can get her a guitar. There's one at the Main Street Flea Market that she's talked about. But when I tell her to get it, she shrugs it off and says it isn't important."

"How about if I help?" He leaned forward a little, and she did a sharp double take, meeting his gaze.

"I don't know." She held her bottom lip in her teeth, and he could see that she was considering it.

"It must be a pretty expensive guitar. I could match whatever you earn."

"And then maybe we could buy the guitar and the case." Brown eyes lit up, and she was smiling again. "I think she'd really like that. She shouldn't have to give up all of her dreams."

"No, she shouldn't." He couldn't explain the way his chest tightened because he wanted Isabelle to have everything, too. He wanted her to have dreams come true and happy endings that made her cry.

But how would she feel if she knew that Lizzie was giving up camp so she could have something she wanted? Proud of Lizzie. That's how he would feel, how he already felt.

"Hey, are you going to come to my Christmas recital for ballet?" Lizzie had switched subjects, and he had to let go of his thoughts to catch up with her changing moods.

Had they made the deal on the guitar? He couldn't decide, but she was standing up, still watching, waiting. And footsteps in the hall meant they were about to be interrupted, probably by Jolynn coming to find her little helper.

"Tell me when, and I'll be there."

"Friday. And afterward Jolynn is having a little party for me. Here, so you can be at that, too."

"Lizzie, I don't think your…"

Jolynn walked through the door, her coral

lipstick bright and her smile welcoming. "There's my girl. Are you ready to do laundry, Lizzie Lou?"

"I'm ready. I was just telling Chad why I'm really working for you."

Jolynn hugged the girl tight, and tears slid down her cheeks. "Lizzie, you're trouble with a big old T, but you've got the biggest heart of any kid I know. Doesn't she, Chad?"

He was a little choked up himself. "Yeah, she sure does."

Lizzie whispered in Jolynn's ear, and Jolynn tossed him another smile. "Well, now, that's real nice."

Lizzie whispered again.

"Of course he can come to the party. He's a part of the family now, isn't he?"

A part of the family. Jolynn's, not Isabelle's.

A truck pulled into the parking lot of the garage. Isabelle told herself she was being paranoid, thinking it was Chad's. She couldn't tell one engine from another. She wasn't a dog. She definitely wasn't going to go running to greet him.

She finished pouring the quart of oil that would complete the oil change on the car she was taking care of and pretended she didn't think it was him walking through the double doors. But he was whistling "Silent Night," and he was the only person she knew with boots that new when she peeked through the crack between the hood and the car frame.

"Hey." She grabbed a rag and wiped her hands as she stepped out into clear view of the man standing next to the car. He'd definitely caught her in a moment when she didn't feel beautiful. Her gray coveralls were grease-stained, and she knew without looking that she probably had a smudge on her cheek, or forehead. Maybe both.

"Hello. I came to give you a message." He stepped a few feet closer, and he wasn't dirty or stained. He was wearing new jeans with his new boots, and a new white button-up shirt. He didn't smell like grease; he smelled like soap and cologne, the kind that made a woman want to hug him, to get close and enjoy the way his arms would feel holding her tight.

She needed to go home and burn her romance novels.

He smiled, and she nearly melted. Why this guy? Why now? Those were questions she needed answers for.

"What's the message?" She got the words

out, and she kept wiping her hands to give herself something to think about other than Chad Daniels.

"Your daughter is working late. Jolynn had a lot of dusting to do. They asked me to come down here and let you know that. And also, I thought we might have that real dinner out. You know, the kind with two people sitting at a table together."

Isabelle tossed the rag in the bucket with the others that she'd have to wash later. "You know they're setting us up, right?"

"I kind of thought they might be, but it was getting pretty dusty around the house, and Larry is at an auto auction in Springfield. I thought it might be a good idea to get out."

"I don't know."

"I have to eat. You have to eat. We might as well go out and get something. Jolynn said the special tonight is some kind of chicken pasta."

"I'm not really dressed for going out." She looked down at the coveralls. "I mean, I have clothes to change into, but…"

He grinned, and then he winked. "If we stand here long enough, I think you'll come up with plenty of excuses for why you can't do this. I think the old excuses, the ones about your daughter needing you at home with her, are starting to lose their validity. She's not at home. She's growing up. Maybe it's your turn to do something for yourself."

If only he hadn't said that. "Chad, it isn't my turn. I still have a twelve-year-old daughter to raise. It's her turn to live, to find her future, to be happy and taken care of. It's her turn to have the life I always dreamed of having."

He sighed and nodded. "Okay, you're right. I've never been a parent. I'm kind of rusty at the whole dating scene myself and what not to say to a woman, especially a woman who is also a mom. I can tell you this—you have a great kid. You're a great mom. You have to eat, and she's already eating with Jolynn."

Isabelle's heart caved. "You make valid points. But it isn't easy, this letting-go thing."

"You have to start, because her growing up isn't going to stop."

"Okay, let me change."

She wouldn't say it was a date. She couldn't do that, not yet. It would take her a while to come to terms with the fact that she'd said yes.

"Shall we walk?" he asked through the door as she changed into clean clothes and washed her face and arms. She didn't have makeup with her, or even perfume. At least she had some lotion that made her feel a little feminine.

"It's only two blocks. I think walking is a good idea. And it isn't freezing cold today."

"The lights will be pretty in the park."

And romantic. Christmas lights, a gorgeous man, and she was wearing wool socks and work boots. So much for romance.

This wasn't the way it happened in movies. But then again, this wasn't romance, either. This was a nice guy taking her to dinner. Her stomach clenched and tied itself in knots. She leaned against the wall, taking a few deep breaths.

"Isabelle?"

"I'll be right out." She rubbed lotion on her arms. And then she looked in the mirror, at a reflection that showed a woman who wasn't getting any younger. Fine lines were starting to appear at the corners of her eyes. Without makeup, she looked pale.

She opened the door and smiled, and he smiled back. He didn't look shocked, or even sorry that he'd asked her to dinner.

Of course he didn't. It was just dinner, nothing more.

* * *

Chad reached for Isabelle's hand as they walked out of the garage, but he changed his mind. She had her heart locked up tighter than Fort Knox, and those walls told him she wasn't ready for holding his hand as they walked down the sidewalk of Main Street in Gibson, Missouri.

"You're buying the Berman farm?" she asked as they passed the park. It was lit up with the Nativity, and around the park were the lighted wire frames of the three wise men, camels, angels and shepherds. A speaker, probably hooked up to the fire station, played Christmas music.

The Berman farm—a house with a wrap-around porch strung with lights and a tree twinkling in the window of the living room. Today Lizzie had shared Isabelle's dreams with him, dreams of learning to play the guitar. Dreams she'd given up on because she'd had a daughter to raise and her daughter's dreams to take care of.

He hadn't ever been the guy that thought too much about his own dreams, not until he'd started getting letters from Gibson. Until then he'd been pretty content with his military career and single life.

"Yes, I'm buying it." He'd already signed an offer for the farm. But he'd also been contacted by the army, asking him to reenlist.

"You don't seem too thrilled." She glanced up at him, a sweet face devoid of makeup and beautiful because she knew who she was.

"I am." He gave in to the urge and reached for her hand. She looked down at their hands, but she didn't pull away. "I'm buying a used stock trailer from Jay Blackhorse, and a friend of his, Cody, is selling me some cattle and a horse."

Did she look wistful, like maybe she had more than one dream, the dream of playing the guitar? Maybe the guitar had been an easy dream to talk about, and to let go of?

"Sounds wonderful." Yes, that was wistfulness in her tone.

They were walking up the sidewalk to the Hash-it-Out, and he could smell the special fried chicken; Isabelle's hand was no longer in his, and he understood why—because Gibson was a small town, and people talked.

He opened the door for her, and she walked through, a little antsy. She waited for him inside. Of course people would stare. He was new in town, and she was the widowed mother of Lizzie, and she didn't date.

Because she had loved her husband too much to let her heart love again? He had spent a lot of time thinking about that, and he thought about it now as the hostess led them to a corner booth. Maybe she had just gotten too busy with work, life and Lizzie to make room in her heart for a man?

She sat down across from him, clasping her hands on the scarred tabletop, once black Formica, now scratched and faded. The seats of the booth were lumpy, and his even had a piece of gray duct tape covering a tear in the vinyl. It wasn't the most romantic restaurant in the world, but he thought it might be his favorite.

He enjoyed breakfast the best, when farmers and retirees gathered at the tables together, having coffee, biscuits and gravy, and usually a good ration of gossip.

"Why are you smiling?" Isabelle was fiddling with the napkin, running slim fingers over the crease she'd made in it.

"Thinking of this restaurant, the people who come here. I think it's at the top of my list of places to eat."

She laughed at that. "The Hash-it-Out?

Not that it isn't great. And Jolynn does make a great apple pie, but really?"

"Really."

The waitress headed their way, slipping past a couple of guys in cowboy hats and dusty boots who flirted as she walked past them. She knocked the hat off one with red hair and told him to go back on the road.

Chad turned his cup over for the waitress to fill. The woman was young and her makeup was too dark, but her eyes were kind. She smiled at Isabelle. "Well, Isabelle Grant, couldn't you find a better place to go on a Monday night date?"

"It isn't a date." Isabelle's eyelids lowered, and she glanced back at the menu in her hands. "We're just friends. I'm going to have a chef salad."

He glanced up as the waitress gave him a knowing look and mumbled, "Uh-huh."

After he gave his order, the waitress walked away, giving one last look over her shoulder at the cowboy with the red hair, the one who had been teasing her.

"Your daughter invited me to her dance recital."

Isabelle looked up and set down the cup

of coffee she'd been stirring creamer into. "Oh, that's sweet of her."

"Do you mind?"

She bit down on her bottom lip, and then she shook her head.

"I don't mind. Of course we'd love it if you could be there."

"She also invited me to Jolynn's party." He sipped black coffee and then set his cup down. "I'm sorry, I can tell her no."

"Why would you do that?"

"Because I don't want you to be uncomfortable. Here I am, in your life because of a Christmas letter your daughter wrote to me last year, and now I'm at recitals, parties, and sitting across from you at dinner."

"I could have said no, but I didn't." She put her spoon on a napkin. "I think we agreed that we would go out and see what it was like, the…"

She glanced around, her lip between her teeth. He followed the quick glance, and he knew what she was thinking. People would be listening, wondering what was going on between the two of them. Being at the café together should have been enough of an answer.

"Right, we did agree to try this." He

winked. "So far it isn't bad, is it?" He wanted a smile from her, something that said she felt it, too, the unexplainable connection. First date, he reminded himself.

"No, it isn't bad, but let's avoid the mistletoe." She shot a glance at the ceiling fan in the center of the room, and he saw it hanging there, from the light.

Avoiding the mistletoe was the last promise he wanted to make, so he winked and she blushed.

When they left the restaurant an hour later, he was still wondering how to get her back under that little twig of mistletoe.

Chapter Six

"What have you decided about dance camp?" Mrs. Teague, the owner of Gibson DanceTastic walked next to Isabelle as they left the dressing room where the dancers were waiting for the recital to begin.

Isabelle shrugged at the question. "I don't know yet. I'm saving money, but a lot can happen in six months. I don't want her to be disappointed."

Mrs. Teague patted Isabelle's arm. "Honey, she'll understand. I just wish there was a way that I could help."

"You're already helping. Where else could the girls get ballet lessons from someone with your experience for what you charge?"

"I'm sure there are places." Mrs. Teague's gaze shot past Isabelle, and she nodded at someone standing behind her. "Can we help you?"

"I…" A male voice, hesitant and kind of shy. Not at all the way he normally sounded. "I have flowers for Lizzie."

Isabelle turned, smiling because Chad was a little red in the face and held the flowers like they were going to bite him.

"You didn't have to bring flowers." She narrowed the distance between them—two steps, and they were close enough for her to smell the roses.

"This one is for you." He handed her a pink rose that was wrapped separate from the other bouquet. "For the mother of the ballerina who invited me. I'm not sure if there is some kind of dance etiquette, but I asked Jolynn, and she said flowers would be nice. And she told me I could bring them backstage."

Jolynn, the troublemaker. Isabelle lifted the rose he'd given her and inhaled the sweet fragrance. "It's beautiful, but we have to go now. They're ready to start."

"The flowers?" He held them in his hand like a club.

"Relax, you can give them to her after the performance. You act as if you've never given a girl flowers before."

He blinked a few times. "Wow, now that you mention it, I don't know if I have. Maybe in high school. Doesn't the guy always get the girl a corsage or something for the prom?"

"I don't know."

She'd never gone to prom, or to a school dance. She swallowed the lump in her throat, leftover pain, bad memories of a childhood that had been spent fighting to survive.

"You don't know?"

She shot him a look and kept walking. They needed to be in their seats, and she didn't have time for him to be clueless now. "We need to hurry."

"Lead the way." He switched the flowers to his left hand and reached for her hand, holding it tight as they hurried down the hall and through double doors into the gymnasium.

"I have seats up front, next to Jolynn and Larry."

The lights went out. She picked up speed, and they reached the seats just as the lights on the stage came on, pink, yellow and green. She slid in next to Jolynn, and Chad sat next to her.

Next to her. She peeked a glance at him, and he was watching her. He smiled and winked.

No one had ever had that seat next to her. It was reserved for family, and she always brought Jolynn and Larry, sometimes one of the other waitresses at the Hash-it-Out. Tonight it was Chad, and as Lizzie danced across the stage, he applauded as if she were his own, as if that girl on the stage was the most special person in the world. And Isabelle knew that Lizzie saw, that she heard, and that it made a difference.

Not for the first time, she wondered what had made Lizzie write those letters. Was it for Isabelle, because Lizzie didn't want her mom to be lonely? Or was it for Lizzie, because she wanted a man sitting in that seat next to her mom?

The thought ached deep inside as Isabelle watched her daughter, graceful, beautiful and so good. Isabelle's throat tightened, and she bit down on her lip, fighting the tears. A tissue was pushed into her hand. She smiled at Jolynn who had a hankie to wipe her own eyes.

"She's a great kid, Is." Jolynn's arm went around Isabelle's shoulder, and the hug felt great, lessening some of the pain that had sneaked up on her.

She nodded and watched her daughter

through eyes that watered, leaving the vision of girls in black and red a little blurry and soft.

As the dance ended, Chad stood, the lone ovation, clapping loud. Lizzie beamed, her smile growing, because this time the man applauding was there for her. Around the gymnasium people stood, joining his ovation.

Isabelle finally took the flowers from him, for fear they'd be squashed. One pink petal had already floated to the floor in his exuberance.

"She's wonderful," he leaned to whisper.

"I know." And it felt good to share that with someone. Someone who didn't have to see how special her daughter was. But he did.

And her heart didn't have to see that as something meaningful, but it did.

"Can I give her the flowers now?"

"Stop being so impatient. She'll be out in just a minute, and you can give them to her then."

"Hey, you two, Larry and I are going to head back to the house and get things ready for the party. Chad, do you want to go with us, or ride with Is and Lizzie?"

"I…" He shot her a questioning look. "Isabelle?"

"You can ride with us."

"Okay, see you kids back at the house." Larry winked at Chad as he and Jolynn walked away.

Isabelle thought about asking what that wink meant, but why bother? She knew how people were. They were always trying to marry her off to someone. And a traitorous voice whispered that Chad wasn't a bad someone.

If someone had told Chad a year ago that he'd be in Gibson, Missouri, attending a dance recital, he would have laughed. A year ago he had planned to reenlist at the end of his tour. He had planned on four years in Germany, doing a little traveling, maybe some skiing.

Instead, he was walking through the Gibson middle-school gymnasium with three pink roses for Lizzie. He had led soldiers, faced enemies and lived with the thought of death and danger. But this one kid had changed his life. He was in Gibson, not Germany. He had a farm, and an appointment to talk about reenlisting.

"There she is." Isabelle pointed, and he followed the gesture, seeing Lizzie as she walked into the lobby, dressed in jeans and a sweatshirt, a bag over her shoulder and her face freshly washed.

"Mom, Chad." She hurried toward them, and he faltered a little, because he was one of the two people she was smiling for, hurrying toward.

That made him a part of her life, in a way he hadn't really thought about before. He was the person standing next to her mom. He had cheered for her after the performance. He had flowers, a little less perfect now, but her eyes were wide as he held them out. She brought them to her face, then she threw her arms around him, hugging him hard. He faltered a little as he hugged her back, and his gaze connected with Isabelle's in a moment that meant everything.

When he drove into Gibson at the first of the month, what had he thought about this journey, his reason for being here? He'd told himself it was about finding a home, a place to settle down, some land.

Maybe it had been about Isabelle and Lizzie; maybe it had been about the land. Now it felt as if it was more about Isabelle and her daughter, less about land. But if he reenlisted?

He wasn't sure he could leave them, or

leave Gibson. Not with Christmas just a couple of weeks away.

"You okay?"

He smiled at Isabelle. "Yeah, I'm good."

"We should go." She slipped an arm around Lizzie. "Ready?"

"Yep, I'm ready."

Chad walked next to them, sharing in a moment that probably shouldn't have been his. But he was a part of it, and he wanted more; more moments, more of Isabelle in his life.

Brisk cold greeted them as they walked out the doors of the school. Snow flurries were falling, light and feathery, barely visible. Chad wanted a real snow, the kind that piled up. The weatherman had promised maybe an inch, no more.

"Do you want to drive?" Isabelle tossed him her keys, and he had to think fast, putting his hand up to catch them.

"Sure, why not?"

Lizzie laughed. "It isn't even a real snow, just fool's snow, and she won't get behind the wheel. She can fix a car or change the oil, but drive on roads that might get slick, that she won't do."

"It isn't nice to make fun of your mother."

Isabelle kissed her daughter's head. "Get in the car."

Chad unlocked the doors and opened the back door for Lizzie, the front door for Isabelle. She smiled up at him before sliding into the car. He walked around to the driver's side and got behind the wheel of the aging sedan. When he started it, he smiled.

"Surprised?" Isabelle clicked her seat belt into place. "I'm a mechanic, remember?"

"It sounds great."

"It is great. It's twenty years old, but I bought it from a sweet lady who kept it in her garage most of the time. She drove it to church on Sunday and to quilting on Friday. The rest of the time she walked or rode with friends."

It was a cherry of a car. A Lincoln with the original paint, original engine and leather seats. It was a boat, but drove like a new car. Chad wheeled out of the parking lot and headed in the direction of the Pine Tree Inn.

He drove down the now-familiar streets that were lined with trees bare of leaves and houses decorated with lights of all colors. The headlights of the car captured the falling snow, and next to him he could see the reflection of Isabelle Grant, dark-eyed and somber, in the passenger window of the car.

There were half a dozen cars in the driveway of Jolynn's. He pulled into the space next to his truck and parked. He hadn't expected a crowd like this.

"Wow, Jolynn really decorated the place this year." Isabelle stepped out of the car and stared up at the house.

Chad walked up next to her, ignoring Lizzie's hidden chuckle as she hurried away from them. "I did this."

"You did this?"

He nodded and surveyed his work. Candy canes, four feet tall, lined the sidewalk. Lights framed the porch and windows. Spiral trees adorned with lights ran the length of the driveway. In the center of the lawn was Jolynn's Nativity.

"I did this. And don't laugh." He reached for her hand.

"I won't laugh." She stopped walking.

It was cold, and the snow was coming down a little harder. Chad stood next to her, wondering why they were standing outside when there was hot coffee and cocoa inside. But he wasn't going to complain, not with her hand in his.

He thought about kissing her, and wondered if her lips would be cold. He wondered if she would slip her arms around him, or stand still, holding her breath. Or if she'd turn away.

With snow falling and Christmas lights twinkling all around them, he bent, touching his lips to hers. She held her breath, but her lips were warm and tasted like the mint gloss he'd seen her swipe across them when they got into her car. She moved, touching her lips to his cheek, and then she stepped back. Her eyes were closed, and a tear slipped down her cheek. He wondered if it was the good kind that came from overwhelming but happy emotions. Or if it was a tear of regret.

"Isabelle, I'd like to take you out again. Maybe somewhere a little more romantic than the Hash-it-Out."

"Chad, please don't."

"Don't what?"

"I don't date. I mean, I haven't dated in years. It feels like a tug-of-war, being pulled between building a relationship and raising my daughter. Lizzie can't take the backseat to a relationship."

"I would never ask that of you."

"I know, but my childhood." She pulled the lip balm out of her pocket and neatly swiped her lips again. "I was the child who was forgotten when my mother dated. She dated a lot."

"Isabelle, I know that you're a package deal. I would never forget Lizzie. How could I?"

"I'm glad you understand. Sometimes I don't know if I understand." She wiped at her eyes. "I don't know if I've ever had a grown-up relationship."

"I know you loved your husband."

"Yes, I loved him."

He hadn't expected his heart to tighten the way it did when she said those words. She had been another man's wife. His heart had never been involved, not like that.

"We should go in." He said the only thing he could think of at the moment. It was cold, and the air was damp. Isabelle was shivering in front of him, and he knew that everyone inside would be speculating over what was going on between them.

"That's probably a good idea." She spoke softly, slipping her hand back in his.

Isabelle managed a smile as they walked through the doors of Jolynn's house and into a world that was Christmas and family and laughter. There were more than a dozen people milling around the large living room, standing in small groups, talking, laughing. Isabelle searched the room for her daughter and didn't see her. But Lacey and Jay Black-horse stood in the corner near the piano, baby Rachel in Lacey's arms.

They were a shining example of a couple that had found the perfect person to spend a lifetime with.

It had to be the Christmas music, the lights, the many smiling friends that made Isabelle want to believe in forever with someone who would love her, someone who wouldn't hurt her. As she turned to go in search of her daughter, her gaze connected with Chad's, and he winked.

That's how she missed the tabby cat slinking across the room. Isabelle tripped over the animal, falling slightly forward and righting herself just before she made contact with a table that held a vase of red roses. Out of the corner of her eyes, she caught a glimpse of Chad as he started for her.

The cat she tripped over yowled and ran under the burgundy sofa.

"You okay?"

She didn't look up, didn't meet Chad's gaze. She wondered if he would be con-cerned or amused. She replayed the moment in her mind and then looked up at him, smiling. Because it really was funny.

"I'm fine."

"And graceful."

"Very." And she was falling over more than a cat. She was falling for a smile, for a man who seemed to know the right things to say.

And that scared her. She had never fallen. She'd been comfortable with Dale, and comfortable with her life here in Gibson, raising her daughter and being a part of this community.

Now, though, she had other thoughts about her future and about life after Lizzie was grown and gone.

"I'm going to see if Jolynn needs help in the kitchen."

He shrugged and stayed next to her as she left the room. As they passed through the doorway, Isabelle looked up, seeing the mistletoe tacked to the wood frame. She sidestepped, and Chad reached for her hand, trying to pull her back.

She couldn't let him do that. She'd fallen once tonight, maybe twice; she didn't need to fall a third time.

"I think we'll avoid the mistletoe." She slid her hand out of his, careful to not bring up the fact that there hadn't been mistletoe outside, just light snow and lights.

"I'll help you help Jolynn."

They walked down the hall aglow with candles in the wall sconces, and his hand reached for hers again. Her heart didn't know whether to freeze up or beat in time to "Winter Wonderland."

She needed to get a grip. He'd come here looking for a woman who wasn't real, who was just the fictional version of Lizzie's mom. Reality was so different.

"You know, I'm not the person in Lizzie's letters." She stopped in the hall.

"Really? I thought you were, Isabelle."

"I'm Isabelle, but I'm real, not the version my daughter fed you. I'm not confident or funny. I'm sure she painted a different picture, tinted everything in pretty colors."

"I think she was honest. She showed me the Isabelle who loves her daughter and cares about the people in her life."

"But I'm the Isabelle who has chapped hands from doing dishes. And a gray hair." She pulled it out for him to see. She knew exactly where it was, because she'd considered yanking it out. "Three days a week I smell like car grease. Four days a week I smell like fried chicken. On Sundays I get to put on lotion and smell like flowers and sunshine."

"I noticed." He leaned close to her ear. "I think you have beautiful hands. I love fried chicken. I especially love flowers and sunshine. And I like the real Isabelle."

She pulled away, because his lips were close to hers. "You like Christmas. You love Gibson, the lights, the people. It's all manufactured emotion because of those things and the fact that you're finding a home to settle down in."

A throat cleared. "Are the two of you going to lurk in my hall all night?"

"Jolynn. We were coming to see if you need any help."

Jolynn nodded her head, but her eyes narrowed, and she smiled a little. "Of course I could use help."

Isabelle hurried away from temptation and into the brightly lit kitchen. The big room had light hickory cabinets, dark granite countertops and stainless appliances. It was a dream kitchen. Tonight the counters were loaded down with food.

Chad walked in a minute after her, tall and not flustered. Since his arrival, his dark hair had grown out just a little. He looked as good in a plaid button-up shirt as he had in that camouflage uniform.

He sat on one of the bar stools and watched as she cut a pie.

Jolynn untied the apron she wore. "I'm going to take a pot of hot cocoa out to the crowd, and then we'll herd them in here to have food. Don't stay in here, Is. This is your little girl's party."

"I'm not going to hide in the kitchen, just going to get a few things done." She glanced toward the sink full of dishes. "And wash a few dishes."

Jolynn was already gone, but Chad had heard. He left his stool and walked around to the sink. As she finished cutting the last pie, he started the dishwater.

"What are you doing?" She walked up next to him.

"I'm going to help wash dishes."

"Really?"

He grabbed the sprayer attached to the sink. "Stop sounding so surprised, or I'll spray you. I do know how to wash dishes."

"I'm sure you do."

He faced her, putting the sprayer back in place. "Isabelle, I do know the real you. Maybe not as well as if I'd spent time here, but I know you. I know that you like it when people offer to help do the dishes."

"True, but the letter was from Lizzie, and she's the one who really likes it when someone else helps me do the dishes. It means she gets out of doing them." She rolled up her sleeves, unable to meet his dark gaze. He didn't let her get away with avoiding him. He touched her cheek, turning her face so that their gazes connected.

"I know that you love your daughter more than anything. And I know that she knows that, too."

"What else did she tell you?" But did she really want to know what secrets her daughter might have shared?

"I know that you love romance, but only in books and movies."

Okay, that was embarrassing.

"I know that you miss Dale. And Lizzie knows that you still cry at night. I know that you counted on him to always be here for you. I'm sorry."

Isabelle looked away, because this had gone too far. It had started out as something fun and light, but the emotion felt heavy. It cloaked her heart, weighing her down.

"I'm sorry, too. But those are small details.

And Dale—" She took the dishrag from him and scrubbed a pan. How did she tell him about Dale? "Dale and I were best friends."

"I've heard that's how to have a great relationship."

She shook her head. "We loved each other, but we weren't in love. We were best friends who promised to keep each other safe. He kept me safe."

She glanced up, wanting to see the look on his face, to know how he took that revelation. Her childhood was a life he couldn't understand.

"I think I understand." He took the pan from her and rinsed it. "It's good to have someone who never lets you down."

She grabbed a bowl to wash. This was so hard, harder than anything she'd done in a long time. "So, now you know the things about my life that my daughter couldn't have shared with you. And I know that you're planning to reenlist. Is there really a point to pursuing this? I mean, you're going to leave."

She had repeated gossip she'd heard at the diner, something she'd promised herself she'd never do. She started to apologize but loud voices carried down the hall and a minute later they were joined by the rest of the party. Lizzie was at the front of the group. She glanced in Isabelle's direction, not smiling. Isabelle wondered if it was her imagination, or if those were tears shimmering in her daughter's eyes.

Chapter Seven

It was nearly eleven that night when Isabelle and Lizzie got home. Isabelle was wiped out. She wanted her bed. She wanted to not have to get up at six the following morning. As they walked through the front door, Lizzie hurried out of the room without saying anything.

She'd been quiet all night and hadn't talked during the ride home. Isabelle tossed her purse on the table and went to the kitchen, lit only with a bulb over the sink. She turned on the overhead lights and found a clean glass in the dishwasher.

"Here." Lizzie tossed a small stack of letters on the counter. "These are his letters. If you read them, you'll know who he is and how much he cares about the people in his life. He's someone you can trust. And I don't think he's going to leave."

"What?" Isabelle didn't know what surprised her more, the challenge to read the letters or this new attitude of her daughter's. They'd always been close, always seen eye to eye on most things.

The challenge in Lizzie's eyes was what Isabelle had seen when three-year-old Lizzie wanted candy that Isabelle wouldn't give her.

"Mom, you can't live your life for me. I'm not always going to be here. I can't be your excuse for not getting involved, for not dating."

"Is that how you see me?" Isabelle filled her glass with water and turned back to face her daughter. "You think I'm avoiding relationships."

"I think you love romance that is safe. The kind in books or on TV. I think you're afraid."

"I'm not afraid."

"Yeah, well, I'm praying you fall in love with Chad." And that was the twelve-year-old, with her chin up and her eyes overflowing with unshed tears. "That's what I want for Christmas. I want a dad."

Isabelle took a step toward her daughter but knew that Lizzie wouldn't welcome a hug, not yet. "Oh, Liz, I want to give you everything. I can do the easy things, like ballet lessons and church camp. I might someday be able to afford dance camp. But I can't give you a dad for Christmas. You can't pick a dad that way. And you can't force two people to fall in love."

"No, but what if this is what God planned? What if that letter to Chad was God putting this all into place for us?"

Isabelle didn't have an answer. How many times had she told her daughter to trust God's plan and to see God in the unexpected things that happened in their lives? And now something unexpected had happened, and Isabelle didn't have an answer.

"Lizzie, I don't know God's plan. But I'm sure we'll know it when it happens. As much as you want this, you can't make it happen."

"Read his letters. Please." Lizzie kissed Isabelle on the cheek and walked down the hall.

He was going to reenlist. Lizzie had to get that.

Isabelle could hear the normal sounds of her daughter getting ready for bed. Water running as she brushed her teeth and then washed her face, the alarm clock being set and then the radio coming on. She bit down on her bottom lip, trying to make sense of what had happened to their lives, their relationship. She touched the small stack of letters from Chad Daniels, lieutenant colonel, U.S. Army.

Closing her eyes, she could see his face, his smile, the kindness in his eyes. She could remember what it felt like when he held her, and when their lips touched.

She remembered what life felt like when someone hurt her. She remembered the pain of abuse. She remembered the foster family that had decided to leave the state and to not take her with them. Dale had been the constant in her growing-up years.

And then he'd been gone. But she'd had Lizzie to raise and Jolynn to lean on. She'd found faith and a Heavenly Father who never walked away and who accepted her as she was, faults and all. She didn't have to be the perfect child to gain His love.

So where did Chad fit into their lives?

Chad drove past his farm the next morning, slowing at the drive, but then going on, because he didn't want to think about what if this had been a mistake. The farm, coming here, Isabelle. He'd never realized before, but he was pretty bad at life outside of the military. That had become clear in the last couple of weeks. In his job he'd known what to do every day. He knew what was expected of him. He knew the people around him and what they wanted from him.

Not that surprises didn't happen. He was trained to handle the unexpected.

Nothing in his training had prepared him for Isabelle and Lizzie Grant. They were a package deal. That was a heavy thought and one that a guy couldn't take lightly, especially when he had just gotten out of the army and he had been single all of his adult life.

He had lived twenty-three years of having his days, weeks and months planned. He liked being organized. He liked knowing what tomorrow held for him. And yet there was something about this civilian life, the not knowing, that challenged him.

He pulled up in front of the Hash-it-Out and parked, but he didn't get out. This town had been in Lizzie's letters, luring him here, to community and people he knew only from her descriptions. Being here had added dimension to their personalities.

Someone rapped on the truck window. He

jumped a little and turned. Jay Blackhorse nodded toward the diner. Chad pulled his key out of the ignition and followed the other man, a cowboy who had always been a cowboy. Chad felt a little like an impostor in his boots that were still new and unscuffed.

"What's up with you this morning?" Jay opened the door and walked through, holding it for Chad to follow.

"I have a few things to think through." Chad thanked the hostess who led them to one of the few empty tables. Conversation droned in the busy restaurant, and the people he knew waved or said hello.

It hadn't taken long to become a part of this community.

Jay scooted his chair out from the table and sat down. Chad did the same, turning his cup so the waitress could fill it with coffee. She smiled at him like she knew a secret, and when she walked away, it was as if she owned the whole world.

Chad shook his head, wishing he knew the secrets she knew. Maybe it would help him make the right choice. But prayer was probably a better option.

"Jay, I'm thinking about that offer to reenlist."

"You can't take care of cattle if you're in Germany."

"No, that's something I can't do."

"If this is about…"

Chad raised his hand. There were too many people sitting too close to them, and he didn't want the rumors to get started. Or get out of control. Since Isabelle knew, it was a pretty sure thing there were already people talking. How could they not? He was the guy that came to town because of letters a twelve-year-old had written. A twelve-year-old posing as her mother.

"This is about me not being sure where I'm supposed to go. I'm going to drive down to the base and talk to some people. And my parents called and asked me to fly down there for Christmas."

Fly to Florida, where the temperatures would hover around sixty degrees, and Christmas dinner would be at the clubhouse restaurant. That didn't appeal to him at all.

The only real tradition his family had was the conference call every Christmas. That was the one time of the year they touched base and caught up on what was happening in each other's lives.

The thought left him a little cold this year,

especially with memories of Friday night still fresh. Jolynn's house, the fresh-fallen snow and people who weren't related but loved one another. He'd had times like that in the army with the people in his unit. In the military they did become family to one another.

He hadn't had kids of his own, but there were a few soldiers he felt as if he'd helped to raise. And he'd learned from a few of them, too.

"Well, you know you have people here who would like to spend Christmas with you." Jay leaned back in his chair, picking up the menu to browse. And Chad knew that the menu didn't matter. Jay had the same breakfast every morning. He had poached eggs, a slice of ham and juice.

Chad had gone for a two-mile run that morning, and he felt a little better about ordering the biscuits and gravy that he had every morning. The gravy was the real stuff, not a powdered mix. The biscuits were Jolynn's specialty.

"I know that I can stay." He returned to their conversation after the waitress left. "But I need to make sure this is what I'm supposed to do."

The cowbell on the door clanged. He shot

a look in that direction, and almost everything he believed to be right fled, because Isabelle Grant was beautiful, even in jeans and a T-shirt, her hair in a braid.

"Yeah, you're not a guy whose guts are tied up in a neat little bow, compliments of a waitress and her daughter." Jay laughed, not caring about the look Chad shot him. "I think maybe you're running scared."

Nothing was tied up in a neat little bow. And if he said he wasn't scared, he would sound like a four-year-old arguing that the dark didn't scare him.

Chad barely spoke to her that morning at the Hash-it-Out. When Isabelle got home, she was still reliving the look in his eyes, the way he'd said goodbye when he left. The look had been one of confusion. She knew how he felt.

She didn't have time to think about it. That was what she'd been telling herself, and she knew it was true. Trying to figure out a man was exhausting. Raising a daughter, also exhausting. Missing him— she wasn't even going to go there. She wouldn't miss him when he was gone.

Tonight she had to wrap Christmas

presents while Lizzie was working at Jolynn's. It was the perfect opportunity to get something accomplished. She made herself a pot of coffee and walked into the living room. But the tree was there, the one Chad had helped decorate. She stopped at the doorway between the dining area and living room, looking at the tree, the star on top. God had planned the birth of the baby they celebrated each Christmas. She closed her eyes, knowing He had a plan for her life, for her future. He knew the emptiness in her heart and the way it felt different now, because of the man who had shown up in their lives just a few weeks earlier.

A man who might be leaving to go back into the army.

Pointless, these thoughts were pointless. She hadn't planned on a man in her life. She hadn't invited this one to show up. And she knew that she'd be fine when he was gone.

She went into the bedroom to drag out the bags of gifts, wrapping paper and tape. She glanced at the letters on her nightstand and glanced away, resisting the temptation to read them.

Instead, she dumped the gifts on the bed. Most were small items that Lizzie had wanted. Hair stuff, face stuff and nail stuff. A cute purse and jeans from the mall—a special treat on their budget. Girls were easy that way. Lizzie was easy. She'd never asked for a lot.

And she'd missed out on so much.

But not love. Isabelle reminded herself of that one major detail. Her daughter had never had to wonder if she was loved. Lizzie had never felt that aching emptiness of rejection.

But she wouldn't be going to dance camp, not this year.

Isabelle picked up the tech gadget that Lizzie had wanted for the last year. Downloadable music. She shook her head, because the world had changed a lot in fifteen years. Isabelle had wanted a boom box as a kid.

Christmas gifts were a special part of the holiday, but feeling loved, that was what counted. Isabelle knew from experience. As a foster child she'd been given gifts, sometimes dozens. But the gifts had often, not always, been empty gestures without love.

She knew that Lizzie had written that first letter to a soldier because she had wanted some young man in Iraq to know that someone cared about him, someone was praying for him.

She remembered the two of them praying together that Lizzie's letter would reach the right soldier. That memory was hard to relive, especially with his letters in her hands. Letters he'd intended for her.

The door opened. She jumped a little and hurried to cover the gifts. But they were all wrapped. Lizzie laughed.

"What are you so jumpy for, the letters or the presents you're trying to hide?" The cheeky kid stepped into the room, eyeing the gifts.

"Shouldn't you be at work?"

"It's six o'clock, time to be home and have dinner with my mom. Are we having soup?"

"No, I thought I'd order pizza."

"Wow, a special occasion?"

"No, a guilty mom who didn't get dinner cooked."

"So, you're going to read the letters?" Lizzie sat on the edge of the bed, smoothing the patchwork quilt that an older lady in church had made. One for Isabelle, and one for Lizzie.

"I have to order pizza."

"I'll order it in thirty minutes. That gives you time to read the letters." Lizzie kissed her cheek. "He's a pretty neat guy, Mom."

Isabelle nodded, because she already knew that. Lizzie slipped out of the room, closing the door behind her. For twelve she was too grown up. Of course, she was nearly thirteen. Lizzie liked to remind her of that. As if Isabelle could forget.

She slid the letter out of the first envelope. She skimmed it, knowing she'd have to read between the lines because a lot of the letter seemed to answer questions that Lizzie had asked. She started at the top, sitting on the edge of her bed as she read.

Lizzie must have asked him if he was a Christian. Isabelle smiled, because her daughter would do that. He answered that he was a new Christian. He hadn't been raised in church, but had attended on holidays. He explained that when he started attending services, some of his buddies accused him of turning to God because he was afraid. He didn't care that they thought faith made him weak. He thought that faith made him stronger. He started to take a good look at the men of faith he knew. They were all strong and courageous. And then he read the Bible and saw that the men in the Bible who called on God were anything but weak.

He signed the letter telling her that it was nearly Easter and he would someday send her sand from Iraq, because it was the land where Bible history happened.

He had given Isabelle that sand the day he showed up on her doorstep.

Isabelle slipped the letter back into the envelope and pulled out the next, and the next, and the next. And through the letters she saw the man her daughter had seen. He was strong. He poured out thoughts about the younger people in his unit and wanting to get them home safe. He talked about not having children, but he had always thought, well, someday.

He told her that he would love to meet Lizzie, because she was the type of girl any parent would be proud of.

Isabelle stared at the closed door, the door that girl had walked through thirty minutes earlier. She was proud of her daughter. Aggravated with her, because she had brought Chad here without him knowing the truth about them, about her. But still, it had been a sweet thing to do.

It had been what a girl would do if she wanted a dad.

Isabelle rubbed her eyes and leaned back

against her pillows. Her daughter wanted a dad. Downloadable music, dance camp and ballet, too, but the real deal, the real thing Lizzie wanted, was a family.

At twelve, Isabelle had wanted the same thing.

But she couldn't welcome Chad in the role of dad *just because*. They weren't paper dolls, where you just grabbed a male figure, dressed him up and gave him the role of husband and dad.

Lizzie needed to understand that there was more to it than that. She put the letters together and slid the rubber band back in place to hold them. When she walked out of her room, she didn't see her daughter.

"Lizzie, are you out here?"

"Yeah, I'm here." She walked out of the utility room, folding a towel. "The pizza will be ready in fifteen minutes."

"Good. Lizzie, sit down." They were in the dining room. Isabelle flipped on the light, and they sat down at the small dinette with the fake wood top, scarred and nicked from years of use. "Honey, I know that you want a dad. I get it, because I know how much I wanted a real dad. But we can't pick a guy out of a hat and stick him in our lives this way. There's more to relationships than that. A man and woman…"

Lizzie giggled and covered her face. "Oh, Mom, please don't do 'the talk.' Not now, right before pizza. I know that I can't pick the guy for you. But you don't pick guys at all. You don't even seem to see them. So I thought if I put one on your doorstep…"

"He'd be Prince Charming and I'd be Cinderella?"

Lizzie shrugged. "It was worth a try. I think I kind of hoped a Christmas letter would turn into a Christmas miracle."

"Let's leave these things up to God." Isabelle stood and leaned to kiss her daughter's smooth, dark head. "I'll run and get the pizza."

"Okay. Mom, I am sorry."

"I know you are. I love you." Isabelle grabbed her jacket and walked out the front door. It was cold, and the sky had the heavy gray look of winter and snow. Chad loved snow, and he'd never had a home, not a real home.

She had learned from his letters that home was the place they moved into on base after the last officer left. His mom had always turned it into a home, though. Isabelle thought his mother was probably a strong woman.

And his dad—an honorable man who didn't want to miss the programs at school; but all too often, he had. But that explained why Chad had attended Lizzie's dance recital and why he'd clapped longer and louder than anyone. Because a kid should know that someone was in the audience cheering them on.

And that moment, when she read those words and remembered him that night, cheering for her daughter, that's when her heart had shifted in an unexpected direction and her brain had told her it was too late to deny what she felt for him.

Chapter Eight

"Is, you have a call from Blane at the flea market." Jolynn held out the phone.

"Could you take a message?" Isabelle nodded at her customers, tourists who'd come to the area to shop at flea markets in the smaller towns. She didn't want to walk away when they were about to order their lunch.

"Can do." Jolynn held the phone with her shoulder and wrote something on a piece of paper.

Isabelle finished taking the order and headed for the kitchen. Jolynn met her in the back and handed her the note. "He has something for you to pick up."

"For me to pick up?" Isabelle clipped the order to the holder above the grill and smiled at Mary, the afternoon cook.

"Yes, for you. Go on over and see what it is. I'll hold down the fort."

"But my customers…"

"I'll take care of them and earn you a good tip."

Isabelle shrugged and grabbed her jacket off the hook. "I guess I'll be right back."

As she crossed the street and headed up the block to the flea market, she got the impression that Jolynn knew exactly what was waiting for her there. But that was okay; it was a pretty day to be outside. The weather had warmed to an almost balmy forty-five degrees, and the sun was out. Christmas was just a few days away.

It should have felt good. Christmas always felt good. So why not this year? She didn't want to think about the reason. Or maybe wanted to tell herself that it couldn't be because Chad Daniels had left town, on his way to a base to talk about reenlisting.

Someone had told her that he would lease the farm for a few years if he did reenlist. It seemed a shame to buy a place that was his dream and then walk away from it.

A bell dinged as she walked through the door of the flea market. She smiled at the owner, a man in his fifties who sometimes went to their church. He walked behind the counter and returned with a guitar case.

"I have a gift that was left here for you." He held it out, smiling big, like he was a part of the surprise. "Here's a note."

"This can't be for me." She didn't want to take it, for fear it wouldn't be true. She knew what was in that case. She had picked it up once before, strumming the strings and then putting it down because she wouldn't let herself dream.

"It's yours." He pushed it at her, forcing her to take it. And then she took the note.

She set the guitar case down, leaning it against a dusty old sofa with gold velvet upholstery. The shop was a mixture of other people's junk and antiques. She sometimes found good stuff in this place: clothes, dishes, even books.

The envelope held a Christmas card. There was a picture of a dog with a Rudolph nose on the front, and she knew that someone had been thinking of Gibson's own Santa when they bought that card. She opened it, her fingers trembling.

Because you do so much for everyone else. You deserve to have your dreams come true.
Love, Chad and Lizzie.

She whispered the two names signed together on the bottom of the card. She wouldn't cry. She wasn't going to cry. She slipped the card back into the envelope and picked up the guitar, holding it for a minute and not sure what to do with it, with a gift like that.

She was used to socks and body lotion for Christmas, sometimes a sweater. Not a guitar that had cost hundreds of dollars, money she could have used for Lizzie's camp.

"Enjoy it, Isabelle."

She looked up, remembering she wasn't alone.

"I will, thank you." She walked out, this time not hearing the bell, not hearing anything. She walked down the street, feeling numb, and then hurt, and then warm, because two people had done this for her.

She walked through the doors of the Hash-it-Out and back to the kitchen, to the storage room in the back of the building. Jolynn followed her.

"Are you okay?"

A motherly hand on her back. Isabelle nodded, but she didn't turn around, not with tears flooding her vision and her heart trying to find its rhythm again.

"I'm not sure why he did this," Isabelle whispered.

"It was Lizzie's idea."

Isabelle turned, knowing there was an explanation and that it might not be one she wanted to hear. "Okay, I can see it being her idea. She is the idea girl. But the money…"

"Is, the money came from working at my place. She told you she was saving the money for camp. The truth is, she wanted you to have this gift. She wanted you to have something you've always wanted. So she worked for me. And Chad pitched in because he was touched by the fact that she was willing to work for this gift when she wants to go to camp so much."

"But camp. She really wanted to save money for camp. I want her to have camp more than I want this guitar."

"And she wants you to be happy. So don't take that sweetness away from her. Don't lecture her for this, thank her for it. You have a wonderful child who is loving and giving.

That's the greatest gift I think a parent could ever receive."

"I think so, too." But this was another way that Lizzie was taking care of her mother. "But I think this shows me something important, too."

Jolynn wiped tears from beneath her eyes, smudging her mascara in the process. "What's that, sweetie?"

"I need to get a life so my daughter will stop thinking she needs to take care of me."

Her thoughts turned, traitorously, to Chad Daniels. She didn't want to think about the fact that she missed a man who had left town a few days ago and had probably already re-enlisted in the military.

"Mom, you like the guitar, right?" Lizzie stood in the center of the living room the day before Christmas Eve, the day before the big Gibson parade. And it was big. People came from all over to view the evening parade. It was the one tourist event the small town could lay claim to.

Isabelle sat on the floor touching up the lace on her daughter's costume for the dance at the end of the parade. The girls who attended DanceTastic would participate in the parade, doing small routines to taped music, but at the end of the parade route, they would do a longer dance.

"Of course I love it." She snipped the thread from the last seam. "And I love you."

"Don't you think it was sweet of Chad to help me buy it?"

Isabelle looked up, meeting the hopeful smile of her daughter. "Yes, it was sweet. It was a kind thing for him to do. Lizzie, you know he's gone, right? He went to talk to people about reenlisting."

"Yeah, I know, but he'll be back. He bought the Berman farm. He wants to raise cattle and have horses."

"I know." Isabelle stood up. "And you look beautiful."

"You're changing the subject."

"Of course I am." Because she wanted Lizzie to be the child, and Isabelle would be the grown-up who took care of her. She wasn't going to tell her daughter how much her heart hurt because Chad was gone, and that she hadn't expected it to hurt.

She flipped on the television, hoping to change the subject, maybe back to Christmas. "Hey, this is a good movie. Let's make popcorn and watch it."

"It's pretty sad at the end," Lizzie said with certain knowledge because it was a movie they watched every year.

"It has a happy ending."

"Yeah, but it always makes you cry. Why do happy endings do that?"

Isabelle didn't have an answer to that. Maybe because of the hope of dreams coming true? Maybe because everyone wanted to cheer for someone to get the wonderful things they deserved?

A truck rumbled into their driveway. They both hurried to the window, and Isabelle knew they were both thinking of Chad. But it was a delivery van. The guy got out of the truck and carried an envelope to the door.

"You get it." Isabelle patted Lizzie on the back. "I'll make the popcorn."

She was in the kitchen when Lizzie screamed.

Isabelle dropped the bag of popcorn onto the counter and hurried into the living room. Her daughter was standing in the center of the room, tears streaming down her cheeks. The delivery van was backing out of the driveway, and a letter was in Lizzie's trembling hands.

"What is it?" Isabelle took the letter as Lizzie sobbed.

Someone had paid for Lizzie to attend one month of dance camp. That someone was Chad Daniels. The letter was signed with a scrawled *Merry Christmas.*

Chapter Nine

Chad parked his truck and got out. The streets were crowded, lined with people. It was nearly dark. He glanced at his watch. The parade would start in five minutes. That meant he had minutes to find Isabelle. He hurried down the sidewalk, away from Jolynn's, and hopefully in the direction of what he'd been looking for his entire life.

It had taken a dotted line, a signature he had almost signed, before he had realized that he wanted to stay in Gibson. He missed the military and the relationships, the bonds of serving with other men and women.

But if he went back, he'd miss Isabelle and, of course, Lizzie. And he didn't want to miss them. He already missed them.

He hurried down the sidewalk, his step light, his heart hammering in his chest like a man about to go into the danger zone, facing the unknown. On his way home— *home,* he liked the way that sounded—he had thought of all the right things to say. At the hotel last night he'd even watched a few of those sappy movies she liked so much. He wouldn't admit that to a single person.

But a guy had to know what to say when he faced the woman he loved and wanted to spend the rest of his life with. Especially a woman like Isabelle, a woman who was strong, tender, vulnerable and beautiful.

A woman with a daughter. That would make him a stepdad, if Isabelle ever agreed to marry him. He had bought a half-dozen books on the subject yesterday. In the end he had left them in the hotel. He didn't need to know how to be a stepdad. What Lizzie needed was a *dad*.

He practically ran down Main Street, because he could hear band music in the distance. He glanced at his watch, knowing the parade had just started.

A few hundred feet away he thought he saw her, a woman with dark hair, wearing a plaid jacket. She turned, and it wasn't Isabelle.

Her cell phone. He pushed in her number, and as he waited for her to answer, he kept walking and kept running through his mind what he wanted to say when he saw her. He slipped his left hand into his pocket and smiled.

"Hello." Isabelle stepped away from the crowd that waited at the end of the parade route. She hadn't expected Chad's voice on the other end of the phone, or his number on the caller ID.

She had hoped he would be here for this performance. She wanted to thank him for the guitar. Lizzie wanted to thank him for dance camp.

Even now her eyes flooded with tears when she thought about his kindness. And how much she hadn't planned on missing him.

"What are you doing?" His voice was soft, and she closed her eyes. She hadn't planned on this feeling. It felt like falling in love for the first time.

"I'm at the parade." She listened, knowing it would only be five minutes before the dancers reached them. Gibson packed a lot into a parade that was a mere one mile long.

They had three school bands, the dancers, saddle club, a dozen church floats and the Boy Scouts.

"I thought you might be there." His voice crackled a little as his signal cut out. "Have you seen Lizzie yet?"

"No, I'm at the end of the route, waiting." She peered down Main Street, and she could see the flashing lights of the town police car. "I think they're almost to me. So, did you reenlist?"

"No. I couldn't reenlist."

"Really? Why?" She took a deep breath and closed her eyes.

"Because I realized that as much as I love the military, there's something I love more."

"What?" Was that her voice, sounding breathless?

"You." And he was no longer on the phone. She opened her eyes, and he was standing in front of her, tall and strong, his smile flashing in a face so handsome, so familiar, it felt like she'd known him forever.

"Oh." Yes, that was breathless. And happy endings always made her cry. But she didn't realize that would include her own. "But you hardly know me."

"I know you." He pulled her close. "I know that yellow is your favorite color. I know you like your coffee with one spoon of sugar and a lot of creamer, but not real cream. I know you love your daughter, and I know that I love her, too. I know that you always cry over happy endings."

She nodded, and tears were streaming down her cheeks. "That part is definitely true."

"I know that I would like the chance to get to know you better, and for you to know me. I also know that next year, I'd like to help decorate your tree again, but I kind of hope that by next Christmas it will be *our* tree."

"I think I might like that, too."

The parade was marching past, and she could see the dancers in the distance.

"I think I might like to kiss you again," Chad whispered in her ear. "I even have mistletoe."

His hand slid into his coat pocket, and he lifted a green sprig into the air. She started to comment, but before she could, he lowered his head and kissed her. Isabelle closed her eyes as he held her close.

"Chad, I love you, too." She leaned against him as her daughter came into sight, dancing to "Silent Night."

He held her close to his side, and they watched Lizzie, together. Together. Isabelle loved that word, because it meant no longer being alone.

* * * * *

Dear Reader

Welcome to Christmas in Gibson, Missouri. I grew up in rural Missouri, and Gibson is every small town that I know. Church, family and tradition are a big part of these communities. It is so easy to get rushed along with the business of Christmas shopping and preparations. For that reason it's important to find those traditions that keep us grounded and help us to focus on what Christmas really means to us and to our families.

I hope you enjoy Chad and Isabelle's Christmas story.

Merry Christmas!

Brenda Minton

QUESTIONS FOR DISCUSSION

1. Isabelle didn't expect to find Chad on her doorstep. How would this surprise challenge her faith and her own thoughts about her future?

2. Isabelle has taught Lizzie to find God in the unexpected things. Is Chad showing up just coincidence, one of those things that happens? Or could it be God's plan, bringing a family together?

3. The people of Gibson have traditions such as the turning on of the Christmas lights and the ceremony in the fire station. How do those things help them to focus on Christmas?

4. Isabelle learned that she doesn't have to be perfect. God loves her, faults and all. How did that change her life?

5. Chad learned that faith made him stronger. How do you think he came to that realization?

6. In life we tend to want to go back to what is comfortable rather than taking a chance on something new. Chad almost reenlists. What pushed him to make that decision, and why was it the wrong thing to do?

Here's a sneak peek at
"Merry Mayhem" by Margaret Daley,
one of the two riveting
suspense stories in the new collection
CHRISTMAS PERIL,
available in December 2009
from Love Inspired® Suspense.

"Run. Disappear… Don't trust anyone, especially the police."

Annie Coleman almost dropped the phone at her ex-boyfriend's words, but she couldn't. She had to keep it together for her daughter. Jayden played nearby, oblivious to the sheer terror Annie was feeling at hearing Bryan's gasped warning.

"Thought you could get away," a gruff voice she didn't recognize said between punches. "You haven't finished telling me what I need to know."

Annie panicked. What was going on? What was happening to Bryan on the other end? Confusion gripped her in a chokehold, her chest tightening with each inhalation.

"I don't want," Bryan's rattling gasp punctuated the brief silence, "any money. Just let me go. I'll forget everything."

"I'm not worried about you telling a soul." The menace in the assailant's tone underscored his deadly intent. "All I need to know is exactly where you hid it. If you tell me now, it will be a lot less painful."

"I can't—" Agony laced each word.

"What's that? A phone?" the man screamed.

The sounds of a struggle then a gunshot blasted her eardrum. Curses roared through the connection.

Fear paralyzed Annie in the middle of her kitchen. Was Bryan shot? Dead?

The voice on the phone returned. "Who's this? Who are you?"

The assailant's voice so clear on the phone panicked her. She slammed it down onto its cradle as though that action could sever the memories from her mind. But nothing would. Had she heard her daughter's father being killed? What information did Bryan have? Did that man know her name? Question after question bombarded her from all sides, but inertia held her still.

The ringing of the phone jarred her out of

her trance. Her gaze zoomed in on the lighted panel on the receiver and saw the call was from Bryan's cell. The assailant had her home telephone number. He could discover where she lived. He knew what she'd heard.

"Mommy, what's wrong?"

Looking up at Jayden, Annie schooled her features into what she hoped was a calm expression while her stomach reeled. "You know, I've been thinking, honey, we need to take a vacation. It's time for us to have an adventure. Let's see how fast you can pack." Although she tried to make it sound like a game, her voice quavered, and Annie curled her trembling hands until her fingernails dug into her palms.

At the door, her daughter paused, cocking her head. "When will we be coming back?"

The question hung in the air, and Annie wondered if they'd ever be able to come back at all.

* * * * *

*Follow Annie and Jayden as they flee
to Christmas, Oklahoma, and hide
from a killer—with a little help from
a small-town police officer.*

*Look for CHRISTMAS PERIL
by Margaret Daley and Debby Giusti,
available December 2009
from Love Inspired® Suspense.*